A LEOPOLD BLAKE THRILLER

PANIC
NICK STEPHENSON

About the Author

Nick Stephenson was born and raised in Cambridgeshire, England. He writes mysteries, thrillers, and suspense novels, as well as the occasional witty postcard, all of which are designed to get your pulse pounding. His approach to writing is to hit hard, hit fast, and leave as few spelling errors as possible. Don't let his headshot fool you – he's actually full color (on most days).

His books are a mixture of mystery, action and humor, and are recommended for anyone who enjoys fast paced writing with plenty of twists and turns. For up to date promotions and release dates of upcoming books, sign up for the latest news here:

Author Website: www.nickstephensonbooks.com

Twitter: www.twitter.com/nick_stephenson

Facebook: www.facebook.com/nickstephensonbooks

PANIC
A Leopold Blake Thriller

Leopold Blake, expert criminology consultant for the FBI, had his weekend all planned out – and it didn't involve dealing with a murdered senator, a high-profile kidnapping, and at least half a dozen near-death experiences.

Three politicians have been murdered in as many weeks, all expertly dispatched, and only Leopold can get to the bottom of it. Unfortunately, as all hell breaks loose on the streets of New York City, he soon finds himself the next target of a powerful enemy who wants him silenced. Permanently.

Against a backdrop of political corruption and murder, Leopold and his team must fight for their lives to uncover the truth before it's too late.

Panic is the first novel in the Leopold Blake series of thrillers, which can be read and enjoyed in any order.

Copyright © 2013 Nick Stephenson

The right of Nick Stephenson to be indentified as the author of the Work has been asserted him in accordance with the Copyright, Designs and Patents Act 1988.

First published in Great Britain in 2013 by WJ Books Ltd.

All rights reserved. This is a work of fiction. Names, characters, places and incidents are used fictitiously. Any resemblance to actual events, or persons, living or dead, is coincidental. All rights reserved. No part of this publication may be reproduced, or transmitted in any form or by any means, electronic or otherwise, without written permission from the author.

ISBN: 978-0-9576167-0-7

Printed and bound in Great Britain by Ingram Content Group, Lightning Source UK Ltd, Chapter House, Pitfield, Kiln Farm, Milton Keynes, MK11 3LW, UK

WJ Books Ltd: www.wj-books.com

Nick Stephenson: www.nickstephensonbooks.com

PANIC
A Leopold Blake Thriller

By
Nick Stephenson

Blake family

From Wikipedia, the free encyclopedia
See also: Blake (disambiguation)

The **Blake** family (/'blerk/ blayk) is an American industrial, political and banking family that made one of the world's largest fortunes in the oil business during the late 19th and early 20th centuries, with George D. **Blake** and his brother James D. **Blake** primarily through Standard Oil.[1] The family is also known for its long association with and financial interest in the New Manhattan Bank, now part of **Blake** Investments Inc. They are generally seen as one of the most powerful families in the history of the United States.

Most recently, since the death of Robert and Gisele **Blake**, the sole heir to the family's business interests, Leopold R. **Blake**, has taken the family's investments in a different direction and has disappeared from the political landscape to concentrate on developing business interests in the fields of modern biotechnology, clean energy, and charitable causes.[2] Although the circumstances following the deaths of Robert and Gisele **Blake** are still unclear, many believe...

Chapter 1

Leopold Blake sighed and removed the gun from the hand of the dead senator. The body lay face-down on the hardwood floor, dressed in an expensive suit, a fresh exit wound to the back of the head staining the dead man's white collar and neatly trimmed gray hair with dark blood. Leopold examined the left hand carefully, lifting it from the floor to get a better view in the dim light. Slowly, he sniffed the skin in long, drawn inhalations and noted a distinct smoky, metallic scent. The forensics team stood back, shuffling impatiently, waiting to get back to work. Leopold took no notice and continued sniffing. Satisfied, he stood and turned to the police lieutenant who was glaring at him from the back of the room.

"Thoughts, Bradley?" asked Leopold, brushing the dust from his knees to the floor.

The living room was spacious and decorated with expensive furniture, although it was in need of a serious cleaning. Warm cinders glowed in the fireplace, the flames having died hours earlier.

The lieutenant folded his arms. "You're supposed to be the expert."

"You look like a man with something to say. What's your take on this?"

Bradley arched his eyebrows, further creasing his wrinkled forehead. Leopold wondered if another fifteen years would have the same effect on his own face, but he pushed the thought to the back of his mind and reminded himself he was still young, if a little scruffy around the edges. The lieutenant paced over to the body and glanced down, taking a second to compose his thoughts.

"Meet State Senator George Wilson," said Bradley, hands on hips. "Records show he's lived here in Boston for the last ten years. Dead in his own living room on a weekday night, with no witnesses and no signs of forced entry. Clearly a suicide. Initial blood work confirms cause of death as a gunshot wound to the head, and splatter analysis shows that the body wasn't moved after death. The bullet we found lodged in the wall matches the gun in the senator's hand, which was registered in his own name and purchased several years ago. There's gunshot residue on the senator's hand where he held the gun, and to top it all off we've even got a suicide note."

"Seems you have everything all wrapped up nicely," replied Leopold. "Why call me in?"

"Standing orders from the commissioner. Apparently the FBI are insisting, and they want you involved on any high profile cases. Says your perspective is useful, though I can't see what use you are here. Open and shut, if you ask me."

Leopold resisted the urge to grin.

"The commissioner asks for my involvement on a consulting basis because I pick up things people like you and your team miss. For example, is it possible you've failed to notice this is the third dead state senator that's shown up in as many weeks?"

"I heard on the news. The FBI said the deaths weren't homicides, and it's not like they're well known for sharing information, so that's all I know. What exactly have we missed here?" asked the lieutenant impatiently.

"Good, you're finally asking the right questions. Can you tell me how the senator managed to shoot himself while he was unconscious?"

"What the hell do you mean, unconscious? That's impossible."

"Not impossible, just unlikely. Observe."

Leopold took a thin penlight from his jacket pocket and shined a narrow beam of light over the senator's prone body, illuminating the various points of interest against the musty gloom of the old house.

"You can see the senator is lying face down on the floor. How did he get there? There's no evidence of trauma to the head, other than the bullet wound, so a fall is unlikely. You'll also notice the dust on the back of the senator's suit jacket and trousers; how did the dust get there?"

The consultant moved the beam of light across the floorboards and continued. "There are patches of floor that have less dust than others – which means the senator was on his back at some point tonight. Dust never lies."

"So what? People do all kinds of weird things, especially if they're suicidal."

"There's that word again. You mentioned a note?"

Bradley nodded.

"Typed, no doubt? No signature? Yes, I thought so. Moving on then, you'll also notice the senator's shoes. Expensive and well-maintained, the sole is worn but there's no dirt. Why is he wearing dress shoes indoors? In fact, he's dressed to go out; but there's no evidence at all that he's left the house tonight. Doesn't that seem a little odd?"

"Maybe. But it doesn't prove anything."

Leopold sighed impatiently and continued. "You'll no doubt be aware that the senator is holding the gun in his left hand – even you couldn't miss that. We know the senator was indeed left-handed; so why were his shoelaces tied by someone right-handed? You can easily tell by the knot. Lastly, look again at the hand holding the gun. There's gunpowder residue on there all right, I could smell as much. What's unexpected, however, is that the senator chose to fire the weapon with his index finger, instead of holding the gun at a different angle and using his thumb."

"What the hell does that have to do with anything?"

"Try it. Holding the gun like that is awkward. If I were going to shoot myself in the head, I'd want to make sure I didn't miss. Using the index finger means the wrist is twisted at an unnatural angle, and is not something one sees in suicides. This man was murdered."

The grizzled lieutenant smirked. "That's nothing but guesswork."

"I'm not guessing, Bradley. I'm observing the evidence and applying logic, reason, and experience to reach a conclusion."

"None of this is proof that the senator was murdered."

"No? Picture it: The senator is in the house all evening and dressed in a formal suit, even though he's not expecting company and has not intention of going out. After dressing, he ties his shoes with the wrong hand and walks downstairs, lies on his back on the floor and then stands up again, awkwardly positions a gun in his mouth, pulls the trigger, and then somehow falls onto his front. Does *that* seem likely?"

Bradley scowled, folding his arms in resignation. "I suppose not. What's your genius theory then, Mr. Blake?"

The consultant paused before replying, lifting one finger to his lips as he considered his response. "The senator has a highly stressful job, enough to cause his hair to turn white despite only being in his mid-forties. A man like that will probably have trouble sleeping. Tell me, was the senator on any kind of medication for insomnia?"

"We found an empty bottle of sleeping pills on his bedside, nothing out of the ordinary. Over-the-counter stuff."

"Any alcohol?"

"An empty glass."

"Whiskey?"

"Smelled like it. How did you know?"

"It helps me sleep too," said Leopold. "So the senator takes sleeping pills on a regular basis and washes them down with whiskey, meaning the killer only has to swap out the usual medication for something a little stronger. Once the senator is unconscious, the killer dresses him and takes him down to the living room, where he puts the gun in the senator's hand and fires a single shot through the head. As a result, toxicology reports will show nothing in George Wilson's system other than sleeping drugs, which would be nothing out of the ordinary, and the whole thing looks like a suicide."

"Why bother knocking him out? Why not just shoot him and reposition the body? Or use poison?"

"Too risky. The killer had to make it look like suicide, which means that as well as making sure there were no unexpected substances in the blood, he had to avoid any evidence of a fight. The killer would have had to make sure the senator was alive when he shot him, otherwise the wound would have bled out differently."

"Okay, say your theory is correct. What do we do now?"

"Run the usual toxicology reports and check for any elevated levels of sleeping drugs, particularly those not present in over-the-counter medication. Try Midazolam for starters. When you isolate the chemical not present in the senator's usual bedtime cocktail, you'll know it wasn't suicide."

"But why would anyone murder the senator?"

"Good, Lieutenant, your second intelligent question of the evening. The vast majority of premeditated crimes happen for one of three reasons: money, revenge, or power. The senator was wealthy, no doubt about that, but nothing is missing from his home, which suggests we can rule out a robbery."

"So we're looking for a revenge killing? Or something politically motivated?"

"Precisely. The senator was in a position powerful enough to make enemies; we just need to narrow down the list."

"How do we do that?" asked Bradley, pulling out a pen and small notepad from his coat pocket.

"I expect you've been watching the news recently. This is an election year, and tensions are running high. Senator Wilson made a lot of enemies by speaking his mind. Find out who has the strongest motive, and you've got your killer."

"Anything else?"

"Yes. Focus on any leads you have on hired killers or mercenaries; this has all the hallmarks of a professional job. With high-profile targets like this, you're looking for someone who can afford to pay for the best. Start by checking out the wealthier members of government with a reason to hold a grudge. Other than that, I'd recommend good old-fashioned police work."

"You're not going to help?"

"I've already helped. You don't want me taking all the credit, do you? I've given you everything you need to get started. If you find any more bodies, let me know."

The lieutenant opened his mouth to protest, then thought better of it.

Leopold stepped back from the body and made his way to the front door, nodding to the forensics team as he passed. "He's all yours."

"Wait, Mr. Blake." Bradley strode across the hallway and caught up with Leopold on the doorstep. "Don't for one second think I'm impressed with your showing off. We would have figured it out eventually."

"I'm sure you would."

Bradley turned to go back inside, then paused. "I'm curious. Have you ever been wrong?"

Leopold looked straight into the lieutenant's eyes and smiled. "Just once."

He walked out into the night, closing the door firmly behind him.

Chapter 2

Christina Logan and her two girlfriends sat at the bar, giggling and wailing along to the music. Suave, the newest mid-town New York hotspot, had only been open a few weeks, and it was still impossible to get in unless you had the right connections. Christina knew this, and had taken advantage of her social status to bag a few VIP tickets for herself and her friends. She looked around the nightclub and beamed a brilliant white smile as she caught the eye of a tall, muscular guy across the room. He raised his bottle of beer in salute and started walking over, smiling back at her as he weaved in and out of the crowd.

The VIP room at Suave was not like your average club. People didn't come here to dance, they came to be seen and they came to drink. Usually by the bottle. The music was played loud and the lights were kept low; nobody wanted conversation and everybody wanted to look their best. Christina felt a tap on her shoulder and turned to the girlfriend to her right – Candice, the one with the sharp nails.

"That guy is totally into you!" Candice shouted over the thrumming music, nodding at the muscular guy as he drew closer.

"He's cute!" Dakota chimed in from the left. "But what about your boyfriend?"

"Hank?" replied Christina. "He's not really my boyfriend. Just some guy I'm seeing. Besides, he's been acting a little weird recently. He said he didn't want me going out tonight. He still thinks I'm back at the dorm."

"Good move," said Candice. "He never has to know. You just concentrate on having fun!"

Christina grinned and began to feel the effects of the vodka from their fifty-dollar cocktails. She felt her skin warm as the alcohol spread through her body, making her smile even more as the tall, handsome guy approached and leaned against the bar, looking at Christina as he spoke.

"Hey, you ladies having a good night? The name's Finn. What's yours?"

"Christina," she beamed and looked down, fiddling with the cocktail stick in her now olive-free Martini. She saw Dakota bobbing up and down on the stool, trying to look over Finn's back to hear what she was saying.

"You in college? You look like a student. Isn't it a little late to be out on a school night?" Finn's voice was smooth, even though he was practically shouting over the beat of the dance track that was playing, and his eyes twinkled as he spoke.

"We're all Columbia Law. Nobody works much on a Friday, so we can sleep in. You won't tell anyone, will you?" Christina said coyly, biting her bottom lip.

"Your secret's safe with me."

"So, what do you do for a living?" said Christina, wanting to know just how many drinks she could expect him to pay for.

"Oh, you know; this and that. Mostly private equity investments, that kinda thing."

"Sounds interesting, I'd love to hear more, but we're running out of drinks. Why don't you pull up a chair?"

Finn laughed and shook his head. He put down his drink, stood up, and took a few steps back so that he could address all three girls.

"Ladies, it's been an absolute pleasure, but I'm afraid I have to be leaving soon. I've got other places to be tonight."

Christina pulled a face in disappointment, a trick that always worked on her father. This guy wasn't going anywhere.

"I'm sorry, I really do! But how about this: I've got a friend who works the doors at Halo downtown. My driver's outside; you guys are welcome to take a ride down to the club and I'll meet you there later. I'll call ahead and have the champagne waiting."

Christina looked to her girlfriends, all of whom seemed impressed, and nodded enthusiastically at Finn. "Sure, sounds like a plan. Lead the way!"

Finn took Christina by the hand and led the three girls toward the exit. Christina stumbled as they went down the stairs, her impossibly high heels not helping her balance, and Finn caught her before she could fall. She looked up into his gorgeous brown eyes and grinned.

"My hero!"

Christina grabbed onto his thick arm with both hands and let him carry most of her weight out of the club and onto the streets. She was looking forward to getting him home later.

The four party-goers spilled out onto the sidewalk, and Christina immediately felt the brisk midnight air around her bare legs; this was not the weather for short skirts, but looking good came with a price and cold legs were part of the bargain. Christina found her footing despite the clawing numbness brought on by the vodka, and unhanded Finn so that she could walk unaided. Dakota and Candice walked ahead, looking around for signs of a town car.

"It's just up here," Finn called out, pointing to the end of the street where the streetlights had gone out. "I'll be right behind you."

Dakota and Candice disappeared from view, and Finn ushered Christina to where the car was waiting, just out of sight of the main road. Except there was no car. Candice and Dakota turned around, clearly confused. *There is no car*. Christina wheeled around to face Finn, the adrenaline now pumping away the alcohol that had been making her fuzzy and slow. Finn was stood still just a couple of feet away, and he spoke slowly.

"I did what you wanted. I couldn't get her alone."

Christina didn't realize until it was too late. Finn's eyes were focused somewhere above and behind her; he was speaking to someone they hadn't seen. Before she had time to react, Christina heard a metallic *thunk* and Finn's head jerked back, a small, red mark appearing in the center of his forehead. Thick, dark fluid began to drip slowly down his face as Finn's lifeless body first crumpled onto its knees and then fell backward onto the road. Christina felt her stomach lurch and she spun around, kicking off her high heels, ready to put five years of kick-boxing training to use. Candice and Dakota were a little slower, still wondering what was happening as a dark figure approached from behind. The enormous man wore what looked like body armor, with thick boots, gloves, and a ski mask. He held the gun limply by his side. The two girls turned slowly as he drew within a few feet and spoke.

"I'm in the mood for some exercise."

The voice was deep and raspy, but strangely quiet and calm. The man dropped his gun to the floor. What happened next was a blur; the man brought his fist hard against Candice's nose, forcing her to stumble back as her nasal bridge collapsed with a wet crunch. A palm edge connected with Dakota's throat, apparently crushing her wind pipe as she immediately fell to her knees, gasping and choking for air. Christina's feet were rooted in place. *Move, dammit, move!* She tried to will her uncooperative legs to propel her away from the horror in front of her, but she couldn't get them to function.

Two huge hands grasped Dakota's head, an arm as thick as a tree trunk across her throat. Christina knew what was going to happen next. With a savage jerk, the man broke Dakota's neck before she could take another ragged breath. He dropped the lifeless body and moved toward Candice, who held one hand to her bloody face, blindly flailing the other in an attempt to work out where she was. The attacker grabbed her loose arm and pulled her in toward him, bringing his knee to her stomach and knocking the wind out of her. He put both hands around her neck and squeezed. Christina could see Candice's eyes bulge in surprise and horror and heard the cartilage and muscle in her neck popping and tearing as the man's grip collapsed her larynx. She quickly fell still.

Christina felt her legs begin to move. *Just a little more,* she willed them, desperate to get away. The man walked toward her; he was only a couple of feet away. *That's it!* Christina regained control of her legs and brought her right foot up fast, using the left to pivot, and aimed her instep at the weak point behind the knee joint. The man blocked her attack effortlessly, and countered by spinning on his back leg and driving the bottom of his heel into her shin. Christina gasped in pain and toppled to her knees. The last thing she felt was a blow to the back of her head, and then there was nothing.

Chapter 3

Police Sergeant Mary Jordan was tired. Damned tired. The call had come in about an hour before, a triple homicide outside a mid-town club. Not her favorite way to start a Friday, especially not at one thirty in the morning and on only two hours' sleep. The gas station coffee in her hand just wasn't cutting it, and she hoped she didn't look as bad as she felt. Mary was attractive enough not to need makeup, but she had thrown on a cursory dash of lipstick and tied back her unruly dark hair just in case she didn't get a chance later, which was becoming more and more likely as she contemplated the scene in front of her.

On the ground lay the remains of two young women, both of whom had probably been pretty attractive before some sicko decided to mess with their faces. One girl's nose had been caved in and her eyes were bulging from their sockets, and the other girl's head was at a funny angle, a grotesque expression on her horrified face. Mary noticed they were both wearing clothes she couldn't afford if she saved up for a year. A few feet further back lay the body of a young male, Mary guessed late twenties, with a single gunshot wound to the head.

"Looks like we've got two killers, Sarge," one of the duty officers addressed her. He was young and puffed up, trying to prove himself. Mary eyed his badge number.

"What makes you say that?"

"Well, this guy's been shot and the others weren't. Two killers."

"Or just the one guy who likes to strangle women."

Mary had seen it before. Some crazies liked to see the life drain out of their victims, liked to dispatch them using their own two hands. They got some kind of sick sexual kick out of it. As for the stiff with the bullet wound, Mary guessed he just wasn't the killer's type.

"Just the one set of boot prints," she continued, "no car, no bullet casings. There was just one guy, and he was a pro."

"Buy why would anyone want to kill someone coming out of a club?"

"You find any ID on these guys?"

The officer nodded, "Wallets and purses weren't taken, so it was easy enough to check. Finn Johnson, Candice Berkeley, and Dakota Hall. Finn's a nobody, works at a nightclub round the corner. Probably knew the doorman, otherwise no way he'd get in. The girls are your usual type, living off Daddy's money and enjoying their college years. Checked immediate family, they're all clean. Not a parking ticket among them. So why would someone want to kill them?"

"They wouldn't. Whoever killed these people was after something else."

"How do you know?"

"Like you said, these guys are nobodies," said Mary, glancing down at the bodies. "You don't see pros like this taking out nobodies on the street. He was after either something they had, or someone they were with. It doesn't look like anything was stolen, so I'd bet on the latter."

"What do you want me to do, Sarge?"

"Tape this place up. When forensics get here, get them searching for any hair or fibers that don't match our other vics and have them call me straight away. Let's find out what's missing from this picture."

The rookie dashed off and left Mary staring at the scene in front of her. This was all she needed, more unexplained deaths. The captain was already riding her ass over a string of high-profile cases the FBI was investigating. Apparently they expected the police to do their damn jobs for them. Unfortunately for Mary, that meant she had to deliver a suspect with at least enough evidence to guarantee a court hearing. If she didn't find one soon, the captain, the commissioner, and even the Mayor would be baying for blood, and she knew where they'd be looking.

Mary swore under her breath and patted down her jacket pockets, looking for her cigarettes. Then she remembered she had quit last week and swore again. It was hard enough to give up smoking without having to deal with this mess. Coffee just wasn't cutting it. Mary bit her tongue in frustration and stalked back to her car, a mid-nineties sedan that was more inconspicuous than a squad car but lacked a decent heater. She turned the car around in the narrow alley and set off in the direction of the precinct, a full night of paperwork ahead of her.

Chapter 4

Leopold saw the blade arc through the air toward his head a moment too late. The blunted edge struck him hard against the padded armor that protected his skull, but he still felt the blow like a sledgehammer striking a stone wall. Faltering slightly, he steadied himself with his right leg and assumed a more defensive stance.

Leopold tensed as his opponent advanced, sword held high. Jerome was forty-six years old, six feet seven inches tall, and built like a pro wrestler. Despite his build, he carried himself gracefully and effortlessly, even with the bulky armor weighing him down. Against his black skin, the dark padding made him look even more imposing, like a deadly shadow. Leopold wished Jerome hadn't insisted on swapping out their usual wooden swords for steel ones.

His sparring partner attacked again, aiming his blows at Leopold's side this time, and he had to parry with increasing speed to avoid a blow to the ribs, filling the empty gymnasium with the echoing clash of metal on metal. The sound only worsened his wavering focus as his arms began to ache from exhaustion. As Leopold's parries slowed, his opponent found an opening and struck hard, connecting with Leopold's ribcage and knocking the wind out of his lungs. Despite the thick armor and blunted swords, the blows still hurt like hell.

"You're distracted," said Jerome through the grille of his headgear.

"I'm just tired. Five A.M. is far too early for a beating."

"It's only a beating if you don't concentrate. I can tell you're not focused. Tell me what's going on."

Jerome lowered his sword. Leopold followed, secretly relieved he would get a few moments to catch his breath. Neither removed his head protection, which was lesson number one in any sport involving deadly weapons.

"I'm trying to figure out the connection between the dead state senators. Three now, all killed within a few weeks of each other. One from Massachusetts, one from California, and one from Florida."

"I remember. It took you all of five minutes to figure out what happened. Staged suicides, right?"

"Right. All three deaths made to look like suicides, all three victims state senators. Other than that, I can't find a connection between them."

"So what's the problem? You'll figure it out eventually," said Jerome, raising his sword.

"The FBI has jurisdiction," – Leopold raised his own weapon – "which means I don't get to know the facts. They're playing a media game and trying to keep me off the team. They've announced that the bodies were recovered, but no mention of the connection between them or the cause of death."

"What's your point?" Jerome began to advance.

"It means that I can't get to the bottom of what happened without going through the FBI staff, who so far aren't returning my calls. There are going to be more deaths unless I can figure out who's behind this."

"Your problem, Leopold," – his opponent circled to cut off Leopold's retreat – "is you just have no faith in other people."

"Thanks, Jerome, but you're my bodyguard, not my shrink."

"Bodyguard? That's a hell of way to sum up twenty years of loyal service. I'm not so sure I should be taking it so easy on you."

Leopold tried to dodge, but he was too slow. Despite years of practice, he could still not hope to compete at the same level as Jerome, who had the added benefit of a lifetime of combat training and expertise.

The giant bodyguard wheeled his blade round with impossible speed and connected sharply with Leopold's wrist, causing him to drop his sword. He felt his eyes water from the pain, but picked up his weapon and resumed the defensive stance, shaking his wrist to get the blood flowing again. His wiry frame was a relatively small target, which he intended to use to his advantage against his opponent's stronger strikes and longer reach. Jerome's attacks were fast and powerful, but so far Leopold hadn't provided much of a challenge, meaning that his sparring partner was bound to grow complacent eventually. All he had to do was focus and wait for the right opportunity.

Jerome advanced again, whirling the blade through the air faster than Leopold's eyes could reliably follow. He counted on his instincts and brought his own sword up to parry, successfully avoiding a blow to the shoulder. The bodyguard countered with a strike to the side of the head, which he also managed to block. He sensed Jerome going for the wrists again and instinctively parried, dodging to the right and following up with an attack of his own.

But he was too slow. His opponent blocked the attack and stepped left, causing him to lose balance and open up his sides to attack. Jerome pressed his advantage and struck Leopold on the upper arm as he stumbled, knocking him to his knees.

"Better!" shouted the bodyguard.

"Hardly. I can't feel my arms, legs, or head."

"You kept yourself from getting hit for nearly two minutes. A personal best."

Leopold stood and bowed. Usually, the first to land two strikes would be declared the winner, and Jerome had managed at least four so far.

"It's over. You win."

Jerome bowed back.

"I'm taking a shower before I regain feeling in my body and it starts getting too painful to move," said Leopold.

"No problem. Don't you need to be somewhere this morning?"

"Yes, I have that appointment later on, but I need to make an unscheduled stop first. This morning's beating has given me an idea."

The bodyguard nodded and followed his employer out. They stepped through into the main apartment, connected to the private gymnasium by a set of heavy glass doors, and Jerome slipped away to make use of one of the many wash rooms dotted around the sprawling penthouse.

Leopold let out a ragged sigh as the pain in his muscles reached a crescendo, before limping off in the direction of his bedroom, where he knew a hot shower was waiting. His apartment took up the entire top floor of an Upper East Side complex, with a view of Central Park to the west that stretched the entire width of the living area, thanks to the floor-to-ceiling windows. He had inherited the property, cars, and bank accounts several years ago, thanks to a trust fund, and had systematically turned the apartment's chic décor and expensive furnishings into something that fitted his tastes a little better. As a result the apartment resembled a bomb site, with books and equipment strewn all around, often in piles several feet high. The only area kept relatively tidy was a small space in the cavernous living room, near the fireplace, where two high-backed armchairs faced each other across a shallow coffee table on which lay the day's newspapers and a bottle of expensive scotch.

Housekeeping staff kept the place clean, but were under strict instructions not to move anything. Food was brought in from one of the many nearby restaurants, and Leopold worked off the calories during his daily training sessions with Jerome, who lived with in a self-contained suite at the other end of the apartment, which he kept in immaculate condition.

There were no photographs or paintings on the wall, only faint outlines where frames had been removed. All the family portraits had been taken down after the funeral and Leopold had still not found the time to hang any replacements. Seeing the portraits brought back painful memories, images of the day he'd buried his mother and said goodbye to the empty casket where his father's body should have been.

The Blake family fortune had sustained a life of luxury for many generations, but since the death of his parents Leopold had no desire to continue that tradition. Instead, his considerable inheritance went into philanthropy, scientific research, and work in the local community. Despite his general distaste for wealth, however, the money only ever seemed to grow, vast investments tied up in everything from timber and coal to nuclear power and military weapons contracts. Such power, however, has inevitable downsides, which is why Jerome was paid to stay close at all times. Powerful men make powerful enemies.

Still reeling from his beating, Leopold stepped into the shower and gasped as the hot water struck his bruised body. Eventually the heat and steam helped ease his pain, and he began to feel human again. Once finished, he dried himself off and threw on a shirt, a ruffled suit jacket, and a pair of jeans, grabbing a cup of thick espresso from the machine as he headed out the door to his first meeting of the day.

He was glad they had no idea he was coming.

Chapter 5

At seven A.M., the leafy expanse of Federal Plaza NYC was already full of people on their way to work, clocking in at any one of the dozen-or-so federal buildings nearby. The FBI field offices were located in the plaza's newest and tallest building, on the twenty-third floor overlooking the state supreme court. It certainly was quite a view. Leopold sat at the back of the conference room and watched FBI Special Agent Todd Coleman take the podium and raise his palms to the noisy crowd of journalists that had gathered inside. The room gradually fell silent and he spoke.

"Thank you for coming this morning. As you already know, the bodies of State Senators Wilson, Carrera, and Hague underwent forensic analysis earlier this week to determine cause of death. I am calling this press conference to announce that the results were inconclusive. As such, we're waiting for more evidence before we can make a definitive statement."

He spoke slowly and calmly. Leopold noticed his suit. Probably Armani, based on the size of the lapels, and at least twelve hundred dollars. His skin was fresh and bright, a product of regular sleep and a healthy diet.

This man clearly hadn't seen any field action in quite some time.

"The FBI would like to reiterate that there is no evidence to suggest that any of the deaths are related. The FBI would like to send our deepest condolences to the families of the victims and offer our assurances that we are doing all we can to bring the perpetrators to justice. I'll now take questions."

Leopold watched the hands fly up into the air as Coleman finished his statement. A deep female voice asked the first question.

"Special Agent Coleman, do you expect us to believe that three state senators turning up dead in as many weeks is a *coincidence*?"

"I can understand your concern, but I must remind you that we are in possession of no evidence to suggest otherwise. Next question."

"Are you saying these people killed themselves, or that they were murdered?" a male voice continued.

"There is nothing yet to suggest the deaths were homicides. We can't take a firm position until more evidence comes to light. I'm afraid I can't give any more specific information at this time. Next, please."

Another round of general questions followed, all of which Coleman answered as vaguely as possible. After ten more minutes, Coleman thanked his audience and left in a hurry. Leopold waited until the crowd of journalists began to make their way out of the door at the front of the room, and then slipped out of the rear exit while the security guards were distracted. He managed to catch up with Coleman making his way back to his office.

"Special Agent Coleman, just one second," said Leopold, matching Coleman's long stride.

Coleman turned, still maintaining his pace. "Who are you?"

"Leopold Blake. Pleasure to meet you."

He held out his hand. Coleman ignored it.

"Blake? What are you doing here? I gave specific instructions to keep you out of the press conference."

"Yes, I figured Bradley would phone ahead, so I came a little early. Nice to finally meet you, by the way. I wanted to see for myself whether you had taken my advice or not. It appears you haven't."

"I'm busy, Blake. There are bigger things going on today that I have to sort out, and I don't have time to worry about this case. Tell me why I shouldn't have security throw you out."

Leopold took a step forward. "Because there are two dozen of the city's most influential journalists in the room next door, just itching for some more dirt on one of the biggest stories of the year. So, if you really don't want to talk, I can always schedule a conference of my own."

Coleman's face hardened and Leopold could see the muscles in his jaw bulge as he clenched his teeth. "My office. Now."

Leopold followed Coleman to his office and sat down on the spare seat with his back to the door. The room was modestly sized, and almost every spare surface was crowded with plaques and trophies engraved with Coleman's name. The special agent took the chair on the other side of the desk and sat partially silhouetted by the light coming in from the tall window behind him.

On the right side of the window hung the blue and gold flag of the FBI, and on the left side hung the stars and stripes. Leopold chuckled softly and imagined himself on a corny television show.

"Something funny?"

"No, nothing. Nothing at all." Leopold wondered whether the man was wearing FBI socks and slept with a picture of J. Edgar Hoover under his pillow. He held back another chuckle.

"You said you wanted to talk. So talk."

"You told the journalists out there that you hadn't determined cause of death," said Leopold. "Why lie to them like that?"

"Cause of death can't be determined, to any degree of certainty, until evidence comes to light that can prove it beyond a reasonable doubt. That's how we work here."

"Yes, that's the official line. I'll catch the evening news for your sound bites. But you and I both know these three deaths were murders. And we both know they were committed by the same person."

"I don't know what you're talking about," said Coleman, scowling.

"I was there. I know a serial killer's work when I see it."

The FBI agent leaned forward in his chair and jabbed his index finger at Leopold.

"Now listen here. The NYPD might have every faith in your abilities, but as far as I'm concerned, there's no place for amateurs in a murder investigation."

Leopold reached into his coat pocket and pulled out a selection of photographs. He turned the first one face up and slapped it onto the table. "State Senator Wilson. Killed earlier this week. Single gunshot wound to the head. Made to look like a suicide, but the killer got sloppy."

"Yes, I've read the –"

Leopold slapped a second photo down. "State Senator Carrera. She was found hanged in a hotel room with no signs of a struggle. Another suicide note, this time with a signature. I also found rope fibers on her wrists, which made me wonder how she managed to untie her hands and dispose of the cord after her death."

"This isn't necessary."

A third photo.

"State Senator Hague, found dead in his garage. This is my favorite. He had apparently hooked up a hose to his car exhaust and committed suicide by inhaling half a tank's worth of carbon monoxide. Problem is, he died with both hands gripping the steering wheel, which is very difficult to do if you're in the process of gradually passing out."

Coleman didn't respond.

"In short: three senators plus three murders plus three staged suicides equals one killer. And you're right."

"Right about what?"

"There is no place for amateurs in a murder investigation."

Coleman leant back in his chair again and held his hands together in his lap. "Like I said, Blake, there's no evidence to suggest homicide, let alone a serial killer. This isn't police work, this is just your particular brand of conjecture."

"I was at all three scenes. There's a consistent M.O. and a consistent demographic of targets. What more could you possibly need?"

Leopold's voice caught the attention of one of the office interns as she passed by carrying a tower of paper files. The special agent waved her away and let out a long sigh.

"We need forensic evidence putting the same person at each scene, a credible witness who is willing to make a statement, or even a sensible motive that fits all three victims. We currently have none of those things, so until such evidence materializes, there's no need to cause unnecessary panic by suggesting there may be a serial killer at large."

Leopold looked Coleman in the eye and smiled. "And that's it, isn't it?" He continued, "You want to keep this as quiet as possible. You know as well as I that these deaths are connected, but you don't want to admit you can't figure out why. Better to blame the whole thing on a lack of evidence, I suspect. You need to trust me, I know you want to get to the bottom of this before any more bodies start surfacing."

Coleman broke eye contact shuffled uncomfortably in his chair. "The FBI will not release statements of record that are based on the opinion of one consultant," he said, in a tone that clearly signaled the end of the meeting.

"You're making a mistake. There are people in danger."

"We're done here, Blake," grunted Coleman, gesturing toward the door. "I have work to do. I don't have time to entertain these unsubstantiated theories.

Come back to me with some solid evidence, and maybe we'll talk. Please see yourself out."

Leopold nodded a brisk goodbye before stalking out of the office back to the elevators. He paused at the lobby desk and leaned over to speak to the middle-aged receptionist, whispering just loud enough for her to hear him over the television that had been bolted to the wall to keep visitors entertained as they waited. A news anchor mentioned something about stolen military weapons before the video feed cut to a busty weather girl for the day's forecast. *Talk about priorities.*

"Madeline, thank you again for your help this morning," said Leopold, grasping her hand and smiling broadly.

"Any time, Leopold," replied Madeline, blushing slightly. "I hope the meeting went well. And thank you again for getting me this job. I can't tell you how much it's helped me out."

"Don't mention it."

"And good luck this morning at the University."

Leopold kissed the back of her hand before saying goodbye and heading to the elevators. As he rode the thirty stories down to the ground floor, his cell phone rang.

"Yes, hello?"

"Blake. This is Bradley. I just got a phone call from Coleman and he's not pleased. What the hell do you think you're doing?"

"I needed to speak to Coleman in person, seeing as how he doesn't return my phone calls."

"Can you blame him? How the hell did you get in?"

"The secret to getting what one wants," said Leopold, "is to have friends in high places."

"What the hell are you – "

He grinned and hung up.

Chapter 6

Mary eyed the clock on the wall of her office and groaned. It was nearly eight A.M., and she hadn't taken a break since she'd been called out in the middle of the night. Her report glared at her from her monitor – yet another case with no leads. Nobody had witnessed the attack, and the area had been wiped clean, not so much as a speck of dust out of place. Which meant Mary had no blood spatter, fiber, or DNA evidence to work with. Which also meant that Captain Oakes would bust a blood vessel when he found out. Mary put her head in her hands and closed her eyes. *Shit*.

She raised her head again and stared at the screen, watching the cursor blink impatiently. Her headache returned, throbbing behind her eyes and squeezing the inside of her skull like a vice. She reached for the coffee cup. Empty.

"Jordan! What the hell is going on?"

Captain Oakes burst into the room, slamming the door into the wall as he came. The cheap shutters on the windows rattled in protest. He crossed the tiny office in one step and slapped both palms down onto the edge of Mary's flimsy desk. His considerable weight caused the whole thing to rock side to side. Oakes smelled of cigarette smoke and cheap cologne and wore a thick moustache that, at this range, Mary could see was stained with coffee. His fat face was red and sweaty, as it always was when he got angry about something. Which was pretty often.

"I want answers, Jordan. Don't tell me this is another dead end? It's my ass on the line right now," said the Captain.

Bullshit, thought Mary. She resisted the urge to say it out loud, but she knew Oakes would hand her over on a silver platter the second he needed to escape blame himself. Instead, Mary drew a deep breath and composed herself.

"Three victims were found dead at the scene. One Caucasian male was shot in the head, two Caucasian females killed by…" Mary paused. "Other methods. The ID checks at the club brought up details of another girl with them who wasn't found at the scene."

"Suspects? Leads? Anything?"

"Not yet, sir. But we're working on it."

"Well, you'd better work faster. I've got enough with the commissioner up my ass about helping the FBI with this dead senator case, I don't need this gang warfare shit hitting the papers as well."

"I don't think it was gang-related, sir."

"I don't give a shit what you *think*, Jordan. Just get me some answers. Find out who the girl is and get me some answers."

"We know who the girl is, sir. Christina Logan. Daughter of New York State Senator Logan."

"Shit. The FBI are going to want in on this one too. Get them on the phone."

"Already done, sir. They put me in touch with Senator Logan's office. His assistant is setting up a call for later this morning."

"You better get me something solid, Jordan," Oakes growled, "I can't go back to the commissioner with another dead-end case. You've got until Monday to find me something useful or I'll have your ass working the graveyard shift for a year. Understood?"

Mary nodded. She was used to working weekends anyway. The Captain grunted something and stormed out of the room, slamming the door behind him. The shutters rattled again and the room fell silent. Mary groaned and resisted the urge to punch the computer screen. Conjuring a solid lead out of thin air was going to be impossible, but she'd be damned if she'd work nights for a year. She had seen what that did to people.

Mary flicked off the screen and screwed up her eyes in an attempt to relieve her headache. She picked up the phone and dialled Senator Logan's office for the third time, praying she could get through to him before he had a chance to speak to the FBI and ruin any chance she had of finding some answers.

CHAPTER 7

The mid-morning New York City sun rose just high enough to peek over the tall buildings that surrounded Columbia University's Morningside campus as ten thousand students, parents, and faculty members congregated on the lawn. The sea of light-blue caps and gowns bobbed up and down as the crowds milled about, waiting for the master of ceremonies to announce that everyone should take their seats. This Saturday morning in mid-May marked the 259th academic year's Commencement ceremony, where the University would grant degree certificates, medals, awards, and honorary degrees to its students and prominent members of the community. The ceremony was due to last until the early afternoon, and tradition mandated that the entire event would be held outdoors on the Low Plaza lawns, come rain or shine.

Leopold hoped for the latter as he pulled on his cap and gown and made his way toward the stage at the head of the gathering masses, just in front of the university's statue of the *alma mater* that looked out over the entire north side of the campus. He climbed the shallow steps to the stage and took a seat next to an elderly woman, probably one of the senior faculty members, who nodded politely as he took his seat. Leopold sat quietly, watching the crowd gather, and wondered how long the ceremony would take.

The view was impressive. The lawns were surrounded on all sides by the grand University buildings, including the dominating visage of Butler Library to the south and the dome of the Low Memorial building to the north. The disjointed murmurs wafting up from the crowd suggested nobody was paying attention quite yet, but the noise levels were beginning to rise.

Leopold felt his cell phone buzz underneath his robe and reached into his jacket pocket to check who was calling. The name Mary Jordan flashed up on the screen and Leopold grinned. *Finally.*

"Morning Mary, long time."

"I hope I'm not catching you at a bad time," said Mary, barely audible thanks to a bad signal. "I need you to meet me as soon as you can. There's been another move on a state senator."

The crowd began to take their seats and Leopold put a finger over one ear, trying to hear Mary's voice through the noise.

"I knew it! Another staged suicide? Or has our killer given up the pretense?" he said, cupping a hand over his mouth and trying not to shout.

"Actually, it's not a murder," said Mary, "but we think it's the same perp. This time we're dealing with a kidnapping."

"Kidnapping? The police don't usually ask for my help unless there's a body to examine."

Leopold's voice was loud enough that the elderly woman sitting next to him to raised an eyebrow. Leopold cupped his hand over his mouth again.

"The police aren't the ones who called," said Mary. "Christina Logan, the daughter of State Senator Christopher Logan, was abducted early this morning, and two of her friends were killed outside a mid-town nightclub. The senator received a phone call demanding thirty-five million dollars in ransom in exchange for her life. Logan asked for you by name. It seems you've earned yourself something of a reputation."

Leopold leaned forward in his chair and took a moment to think. "I'm in the middle of something right now. Sounds simple enough for the police to handle," he said, eventually.

"Just hang on, I'm getting to the good bit," said Mary, her voice getting more animated. "The senator received the ransom demand yesterday, two hours before Christina disappeared. Now he can't get hold of the kidnapper to agree to an exchange."

Leopold sat up straight. She had his attention. "Okay, you've given me something to think about," he said. "Tell Senator Logan I'll take a look. When does he want to speak?"

"The senator wants to meet you today. In two hours. I'll text you the address; just meet me there."

"Good. I'll make my way over there as soon as I can. There's just something I have to take care of first."

Mary hung up. Leopold stood and walked to the front of the stage, where the Master of Ceremonies was checking the microphone and leafing through his script.

He could feel the eyes of the elderly woman with the raised eyebrows on his back.

"Excuse me." he tapped the robed man on the back of the shoulder.

"Mr. Blake, hello! Good to see you here bright and early! What can I do for you?"

"Something's come up, I'm afraid. Have to go. Please give my apologies to the Dean," said Leopold, turning to leave.

"Something more important than receiving a doctorate from one of the world's leading universities?"

"Honorary doctorate, actually," he replied, "and yes, I'm afraid so. Please be kind enough to drop it in the mail. Thank you."

He walked briskly away before the old man had a chance to respond, and texted Jerome to come and pick him up. He made his way down the steps and onto the lawns, squeezing his way through the thick crowd of students and parents. After a few minutes of jostling, Leopold finally made it off the campus and onto the street. Jerome arrived thirty seconds later and pulled the dark Bentley Mulsanne to the side of the road. Leopold pulled open the rear passenger door and slipped inside. He updated the bodyguard on the conversation with Mary, and they set off toward the senator's East Hampton address.

"How do you know it's the same guy?" said Jerome, turning his head.

"Who else would target a senator's daughter on US soil? There are definitely easier targets. This is clearly someone trying to send a message."

"What message?"

"That's the thirty-five million dollar question. I'll know more after a chat with the senator. How fast can you get us there?"

"It's maybe two hours," said Jerome, "but once we get out of the city I can probably make up for lost time."

"Good. Don't be afraid to put your foot down."

Once free of the New York City traffic, the Mulsanne glided effortlessly through the Suffolk County back roads, lined on either side with green trees and a horizon specked with the occasional gated community and small town. Despite the ultra-high spec of the Mulsanne, Leopold hadn't been able to help adding his own touches to the car's cabin. In addition to the standard features, he had installed a wireless system that could sync directly with his cell phone and add extra functionality – such as call tracing, digital encryption, and satellite connectivity to ensure he always had a signal. Leopold always made sure he had the best equipment money could buy, and his money could buy a hell of a lot.

Jerome turned on the radio and tuned into a news channel to pass the time. The two men whose voices came through the Bose speaker system were discussing the stolen military weapons story, and the conversation was getting heated. He asked Jerome to turn up the volume. According to a reliable source, one of the men claimed, a large supply of prototype explosives had been stolen from a secure facility in Maryland three days before, and the authorities were at a loss as to how it had happened. Leopold wondered whether this was what had put Coleman in such a bad mood. The news story was cut short as the commercials started playing.

Leopold pulled his cell phone out of his coat pocket and noticed a missed call from an unknown number, probably Mary leaving another message about the case. He dialed his voicemail and punched in his access code, absent-mindedly rubbing his temple in an effort to numb a sudden headache. The morning's workout hadn't been kind to him, and he was looking forward to finishing the meeting with the senator as soon as possible and taking a long, hot bath. But that would have to wait. The electronically altered voice that greeted him wasn't Mary:

Good morning, Mr. Blake, I notice you've been taking quite an interest in my recent work. I'm flattered by the attention, but I'm afraid this is where the fun has to stop. I look forward to finally meeting you in person, although I expect the feeling won't be mutual.

Leopold frowned and hooked his cell phone up to the car's wireless stereo system. After a few seconds, the devices synced and he cranked up the volume.

"Jerome, what do you think of this?" He played back the message through the car's speakers.

"I'll run the tracer and see where it leads," said the bodyguard. "You do remember I told you to keep this cell phone number private, don't you?"

"Yes, of course. I haven't shared it with anyone. Even Mary has to dial through a password-protected proxy to get through. Looks like whoever called me didn't want to be found."

"He probably just used a scrambled line," said Jerome, pressing a series of keys on the car's touchscreen panel. "The system will work out the origin of the signal eventually. It'll only take a minute."

"Unless he's used a scrambled signal. In which case we've got no chance of tracking it."

"Hang on. We've got company," said Jerome, putting both hands back onto the wheel.

Leopold turned in his seat and looked out the rear window. A black SUV was approaching fast, straddling both lanes of the road. He could make out at least two people inside, although the windshield was slightly tinted so he couldn't be sure. He could hear the roar of the SUV's engine as it approached, straining to beat the pace of the Mulsanne.

"Hold on," said Jerome, planting his right foot to the floor.

The Bentley surged forward, carried by the huge twin-turbo V8 engine under the hood, and the SUV started to fall behind. The bodyguard eased the car around the winding roads, letting the speed fall slightly to avoid throwing them into a ditch. The SUV kept pace, then began to gain ground again as they found themselves on a long stretch of road where the Bentley's precise handling was no advantage. The noise of the Mulsanne's engine filled the cabin as the car sailed forward, pulling away from the SUV by a few feet. Leopold turned to face the front and saw the speedometer hit ninety miles per hour, ninety five. One hundred. Then he saw the bend approach.

Jerome steered into the turn and the Mulsanne's computer-assisted traction control kicked in. The system engaged the rear brakes for a split second and sent more power to the outer wheels, helping guide the heavy chassis round the tight corner. Unfortunately, the SUV had no intention of making the turn, and increased its speed on approach. Leopold already knew what would happen next. He felt the car lurch forward with a deafening crunch as the other vehicle slammed into their back, sending the Bentley spinning out of control. He heard the sound of screeching metal and then there was darkness.

CHAPTER 8

The first thing Leopold noticed when he woke was the smell of gasoline and metal. As his ears began to function he could hear the Bentley's chassis groaning under its own weight and the sound of footsteps crunching through broken glass. His vision returned, and he could just about make out the still body of Jerome in the driver's seat and realized the car had been tipped upside down. He heard the door wrench open and felt a strong grip pull him out onto the road by his ankles. Fading in and out of consciousness, he saw the same thing happen to Jerome.

"Is he alive?"

Leopold made out the husky voice, though he couldn't see whom it belonged to. From the accent he guessed its owner was Eastern European, probably Czech.

"Looks like it," said another voice.

"Good. We can have some fun."

He felt a kick to his side and let out a gasp. The two men jeered and positioned themselves at either end of his body, one grabbing him by the arms and the other supporting his legs. They hoisted him off the road and effortlessly carried him over to the SUV, tossing him into the back seat. The door slammed close to his face, causing him to finally snap out of his daze and sit up. His headache had suddenly gotten a lot worse. He stared at the two men, fixing their faces in his mind. Both were a little over six feet tall, with shaved heads and arms as thick as their legs. Imposing, but not in the same league as Jerome. Both carried handguns tucked into their jeans and both had an assortment of tattoos on their bulging forearms. They glared back menacingly, showing their yellow teeth, close enough for their breath to fog the glass. Leopold looked over to where Jerome had been lying. He had vanished.

The two men must have sensed something was wrong and immediately turned to where the bodyguard had been seconds earlier, expressions of confusion on their ragged faces. They stalked over to the upturned Bentley and drew their weapons, searching for their prey. One of the men stepped toward the front of the car and peered around the crumpled hood. That was when Jerome attacked. The bodyguard's palm connected with the man's throat, choking him as his larynx collapsed and his airways filled with blood. In the split second it took the injured man to realize what had happened, Jerome grasped his forearm, turned on his heel, and flipped the man over his shoulders with such force that Leopold heard him shriek as he smashed into the road.

He watched the giant bodyguard quickly bring his palm down onto the man's elbow while pulling the wrist upwards, snapping the arm. The Czech squealed in pain and horror as bone sliced through his tattooed skin, falling silent as Jerome slammed his skull into the asphalt. Grabbing the unconscious man's firearm, Jerome raised the weapon level with the other attacker and fired, just as the second assailant brought his own gun up to take a shot. His head exploded in a mist of crimson and he dropped to the ground, just a few feet away. Leopold saw Jerome lean in closer to the first man, checking for a pulse, before walking back to the SUV and opening the door to help his employer out onto the road. Leopold took a moment to look up at the towering bodyguard, whose features had softened.

"I'm fine, don't worry," said Leopold, noticing the look of concern. "Who were those guys?"

"Didn't get a chance to ask, I'm afraid."

"Well, I don't think we'll get any useful information out of this guy," said Leopold, pointing at the body lying nearby. "What about the other one?"

"No pulse. Blood loss and head trauma were too much for him."

"And you didn't think it might be a good idea *not* to kill both of them? The police are going to be swarming all over the place. This looks like an execution. Not exactly self-defence."

"Relax. It's my job to keep you alive, so if I'm in any doubt I put your safety first. It's an unfortunate outcome, but it's manageable. Let me handle the cleanup."

"Fine, but be quick," said Leopold, turning his attention to the ruined Bentley. "We're already late as it is."

Chapter 9

The black Mercedes S65 AMG swept silently through the quiet East Hampton roads. Mary sat in the back, fully insulated from the outside world, and soaked up the view. Impossibly huge houses sailed past on either side, most of which were set back from the road and locked up behind heavy metal gates. Each house sat on acres of pristine lawn and most were nestled close to the woodland areas that seemed to stretch all the way out to the horizon. One or two had security guards standing in plain view by the front door.

"Not far to go now, ma'am," said the driver, turning his head.

Mary nodded and pulled out a small makeup mirror. She adjusted her hair and added some foundation to the dark circles under her eyes. The result was just about acceptable, but hopefully the senator wouldn't be looking too closely. Not with everything he had to worry about, anyway.

The car pulled around a corner and the houses disappeared, leaving just an empty road lined with trees. After thirty seconds they reached a clearing to the right and a set of large iron gates. The car pulled up and the driver opened his window, leaning out of it to reach the keypad mounted near one of the pillars. He punched in a code and the gates jostled open, swinging slowly backward to allow the car passage. Mary couldn't make out a house yet, only a long driveway lined with trees and immaculately trimmed bushes.

"Just half a mile or so to the house, ma'am," said the driver, as he started the car moving again.

Mary had assumed that the senator had money, but she hadn't expected him to own a large estate in one of the most expensive neighborhoods in the world. She couldn't help but feel slightly intimidated, but quickly shrugged it off and concentrated on what she was planning to say during the meeting.

Mary had been surprised that the senator had agreed to see her at such short notice. Usually, the NYPD was kept out of the loop in high-profile cases like this, especially when the FBI got wind of what was going on and started fencing other departments out. This time felt different though, and the veteran police sergeant wasn't sure what the senator was expecting from her. He had sounded a little distant on the telephone, a little distracted. Mary supposed that was probably a normal reaction to finding out your only daughter had been kidnapped by a violent psychopath, but there was something niggling at the back of her mind. Something just didn't feel right, but she couldn't work out what it was. Hopefully, Leopold would be able to shed some light on the situation. As usual.

The senator's house loomed into view, and the Mercedes rolled up to the front door. The asphalt gave way to white gravel and the tires crunched quietly over the neatly raked stones before stopping near the entrance archway. The driver stepped out of the car and rang the doorbell. One of the house staff answered, a middle-aged man in a smartly pressed uniform, who said a few words to the driver that Mary couldn't quite make out. The driver nodded and opened the rear passenger door for her, tipping his cap as she climbed out and went inside the house. The front door opened up into the entrance hall, an enormous atrium clad in white marble, with ceilings that stretched a full three stories into the air. Mary saw another man walking toward her, dressed in a dark blue uniform and body armor, with a large handgun holstered to his hip. It looked like a .45 SIG Sauer.

"Senator Logan is upstairs at the moment, ma'am," said the security guard, drawing up close enough that she could smell his cheap cologne. "Perhaps you would be comfortable waiting in the drawing room? The senator will come down when Mr. Blake has arrived."

Mary took a second to look the man up and down, a force of habit from years of sizing up potentially dangerous suspects on the force. She could tell he carried at least one other concealed handgun, and probably a bladed weapon sheathed to his calf, judging by the cut of the trousers. His face was pockmarked and scarred, suggesting occupational damage, and his expression was passive. His eyes gave away nothing. This guy was clearly a pro, but probably not in charge. That meant there must be others.

"He's not here yet?" said Mary, trying to sound casual. "Okay, I'm sure the drawing room will be fine, thank you."

"I'm sure they won't be long getting here, ma'am."

The security guard, whose name tag identified him as Viktor, led Mary through several long hallways before they arrived at a large, plush room with four luxurious armchairs positioned to face the open fireplace on the back wall. Another guard stood at the window, who turned to greet them as they entered. This man was of similar build to Viktor, but a few inches taller, with a shock of white-blond hair instead of the crew cut that Viktor wore.

"Please, sit," said the blond.

Mary took a seat in one of the soft armchairs, and Viktor left the room without a word. She turned to look at the blond, who was also clearly carrying a multitude of hidden weaponry, and checked his name tag. She smiled.

"So, your name's Dolph?" she asked. "Like Lundgren? Did your parents have a sense of humor?"

Dolph didn't respond, but Mary was sure his blank expression flickered momentarily. Probably best not to test the patience of a heavily armed security guard who looked like he could punch through walls. She turned away and pulled out her cell phone. No calls yet.

Mary hoped Leopold would get there soon. He would arrive, no doubt, with some insane theory about the case and a list of unlikely leads to chase up. Not a shred of evidence of course, but Mary could usually rely on him to get results. At least professionally. On a personal level, Mary didn't even know where to begin with Leopold, but she knew that life was always a little more interesting when he was around. She smiled to herself and kept her eyes on the door.

Chapter 10

Jerome pulled the crumpled SUV up to the set of heavy iron gates that shielded the senator from members of the general public. He announced their arrival on the intercom and the gates swung open slowly, creaking and groaning under their own weight. They were greeted at the front door by the senator himself, his face drawn and his eyes puffy. He looked like he had been awake for days.

"Oh good, you're here, please come in," said Senator Logan, pulling the door back and gesturing for them to come through.

Leopold stepped into the hallway and looked around, noticing the pristine marble and ornate staircase that wound its way up to the first floor, a good twenty feet above ground level. Leopold could make out the master bedroom upstairs through an open door and noticed the bed was still unmade. All the other doors were closed. Several uniformed guards stood in strategic positions throughout the upper levels, each wearing bullet-proof vests and what looked like SIG Sauer handguns holstered at the hip. Two of the security officers stood on the staircase, standing to attention.

"I'd like to introduce you to the head of my security team." Logan gestured to the largest of the two men. "This is Jack Stark; ex-military man. Tours in Afghanistan and Iraq, I believe."

Stark nodded dispassionately. He stood a little shorter than Jerome at around six feet four inches, but was just as muscular and looked a little younger. On his forearm was a tattooed insignia with something written underneath, but Leopold couldn't quite make out the words.

"And this is Viktor Baikov," continued the senator. "He reports directly to Stark and takes care of the day-to-day running of things around here."

Viktor grunted in response but otherwise made no sign that he had heard what the senator had said.

"I decided to hire a third party to keep an eye on me," Logan continued. "The police and the FBI can only do so much to keep me safe, and I'd rather put my life in the hands of someone earning more than minimum wage."

"Keep you safe from what, Senator?" said Leopold.

"We both know what's going on here, Mr. Blake. I know what they're peddling in the news, but I didn't get to where I am today without having contacts in all the right places."

"I'm not sure I know what you mean."

"Let's just say the FBI should listen more carefully to your theories."

"And just what would those theories be?"

"Don't underestimate me, Mr. Blake," said Logan. "I found out about Wilson before you even got the call, and I had Stark's team installed last week after reading your reports on Carrera and Hague. There's clearly a pattern, whatever the FBI might think."

"That's very prudent of you," said Leopold.

"I checked Stark's references and hired him on the spot. He's certainly impressed me so far. Isn't that right, Stark?"

"It's my job, sir," said Stark, keeping his eyes on Leopold.

They left Viktor and Stark on the stairs, and the senator led the group through a wide hallway that separated the entrance hall from the rest of the house. On the walls hung numerous framed photos, mostly from publicity events and press appearances the senator had attended through the years. Leopold noticed one in particular and stopped to look closer.

"Ah, a personal favorite of mine," said Logan.

Leopold looked at the black-and-white photograph of the senator shaking hands with the president of the United States at a birthday celebration. The two men were both grinning with wide, bright smiles. A half-eaten cake was on the table in front of them, and a large banner was hanging in the background, the number fifty-three written in large, glittering letters across its width.

"Whose party was this?" asked Leopold.

"Oh, the president and I go way back. This was taken at his fifty-third birthday a couple of years ago. Most people notice that one; I've seen Stark staring at it a few times. Follow me."

Logan ushered them through to a large room, with several empty armchairs arranged around the fireplace. Mary Jordan sat in the corner, dressed in civilian clothes, a look of impatience on her face. An enormous blond security guard stood by the window.

"Sorry we're late," Leopold offered. "Traffic was murder."

Mary didn't reply. The consultant settled himself into one of the armchairs and Jerome sat down near Mary, his weight straining the delicate sofa's wooden frame. The senator took a seat in the remaining armchair opposite Leopold, took an unopened bottle of scotch and a crystal tumbler from the nearby cabinet, unsealed the whisky, and poured himself a healthy measure. He kept the bottle with him, leaving the drink cabinet empty save for a spare glass that had accumulated a thin layer of dust.

"Senator, I need to ask you some questions," said Leopold, waiting for Logan to fill his glass. "Do you know of anyone who would have a motive to harm to you or your family?"

"No doubt the same person who killed Carrera, Wilson, and Hague," said Logan, taking a short sip of scotch.

"Why kidnapping? The other victims were murdered. It's unusual to see a killer change their approach like this."

"That's why Stark and his men are here," said the politician, gesturing at Dolph. "With a team of eighteen highly trained security personnel on standby, nobody would be stupid enough to try coming after me direct. Instead, they come at me through my daughter. Like the cowards they are."

"Do you have any idea why someone would want to get to you?" said Leopold.

"Could be anything. A man in my position makes a lot of enemies. Clearly money is a motive here."

"Why do you say that?"

"The kidnapper asked for money. I would have thought his motivation would be obvious," said Logan, the pitch of his voice raised in irritation.

"Not all kidnappings are financially motivated," said Leopold. "And we know that the call came in a full two hours before Christina was seen leaving the nightclub early this morning. How do you explain that?"

"I can't speak to the mind of a lunatic," said the politician, drinking deeply from his glass of scotch. "Maybe he thought he wouldn't have any issues grabbing her and wanted to catch me before I fell asleep for the night. Set the wheels in motion. Thirty-five million dollars is a lot of money to get hold of; it takes time."

"Tell me about the arrangements for the exchange. Were the police notified?"

"Of course. In order to arrange for that much cash to be delivered, I had to inform my insurance company. I have a specific policy in place for situations like this, and they'll cover any ransom money paid over to the kidnapper, on the condition that the authorities are informed," said Logan, draining the last of his scotch. "Fortunately I have enough pull at the mayor's office to get the NYPD to back off; otherwise, they'd insist on leading the investigation themselves. I've allowed Ms. Jordan to be present, on the condition that she bring you too. I made it clear I wanted a specialist to look into this, which is why you're here."

"What happened next?" asked the consultant, arching his fingers and leaning forward.

"I told the kidnapper that I could deliver the cash anywhere he wanted, but that I needed to speak to my daughter first, to prove she was alive. He agreed and we arranged to speak again by telephone to organize the exchange. The call was supposed to be at five this morning, but it never came. And now they've both disappeared off the face of the Earth."

"Did you recognize the kidnapper's voice?"

"No, his voice was electronically altered."

"Christina is in college. Columbia, I assume?" said Leopold, looking into Logan's eyes.

"Yes, she's a senior there. How did you know?" said the senator, his eyes flicking away back to the bottle of liquor on the nearby table.

"We know she lives in New York, and Columbia is the best the state has to offer, so naturally I took a shot. Can you tell me the names of any of her close friends at college? We'll need to speak with them immediately."

"Of course. Stark and his team have been kind enough to brief me fully on my daughter's friends. I have to make sure she's moving in the right circles, you understand."

The senator rose from his chair, scribbled a few names on a piece of note paper, and handed it to the consultant, who folded it and placed it inside his jacket pocket.

"Thank you," said Leopold. "We'll get in touch when we know more."

"That's it?" said Logan. "You don't need anything else?"

"I've seen plenty already, thank you," replied Leopold, turning to leave. "We'd better get going."

"Wait a minute. I insist you take Stark with you. If there's some madman out there, you'll need some protection. I'll be traveling into Manhattan later this afternoon, so we can arrange to meet again later. I'll be at my townhouse in Park Slopes," said Logan.

"No need, I have my own security." Leopold gestured toward Jerome. "We'll call you when we have an update."

He noticed the senator's jaw clench. They each rose from their seats said goodbye to the senator, who insisted that Dolph escort them back outside. The blond security guard shut the heavy door behind them as they stepped out onto the gravel driveway and up to the ruined SUV that sat waiting for them.

"Nice ride," said Mary. "Any chance you want to tell me what happened?"

"I'll tell you on the way. Jump in," said Leopold.

Mary got into the back seat. Leopold and Jerome sat in the front and shut the doors. The bodyguard started the engine and they rolled back in the direction of the main road.

"Did you get everything you needed?" asked Mary.

Leopold turned and nodded. "Enough to know he was lying through his teeth."

Chapter 11

Colonel Jack Stark watched Dolph shut the heavy front door and brushed away the pang of anger that came over him. It wasn't like the senator to have visitors without clearing it with him first. This was a definite security breach. He would have to make sure it didn't happen again.

"Can you confirm our guests have left the perimeter?" said Stark, holding a finger up to the tiny speaker in his ear.

"Affirmative." The voice over the earpiece was clear, as though the person speaking were standing close by.

Good. Stark was always uneasy when the senator had visitors; there was too much at stake to allow people into the house who hadn't been through a full security sweep. That applied double to cops and trained bodyguards.

"Stark, Viktor. I need you to keep tabs on Blake and the others," the senator's voice echoed down the hallway as he approached.

"Yes, sir," said Stark, turning to Viktor. "Get the comms team to keep the tracer running at all times. Report back every thirty minutes."

Viktor nodded once and marched away upstairs and out of sight. Stark turned back to face the senator.

"We planted a tracker on their vehicle after they arrived," explained Stark. "We can trace them wherever they go to within a couple of meters. If they get out of the car, we can follow them on foot. I'll send a small team."

"Very impressive," said Logan.

"It's standard protocol, sir," replied Stark.

"Make sure you keep Blake in your sights at all time. I want regular updates, and inform me immediately if he sticks his nose in where it doesn't belong."

"Yes, sir. Just like we discussed."

"Good. And don't forget we have one more set of guests arriving before we head back to the city. I want you to make sure they don't try anything stupid while they're in my house. Understand?"

Stark nodded and watched the senator return upstairs. He called Dolph over from his position by the door.

"Take four men and keep a tail on Blake and the others. Take two cars in case they split up. Report in every thirty minutes, and once you get into the city, keep them in sight at all times. And get Vinnie down here. I need to brief him on our next set of visitors."

Dolph confirmed his orders and stalked off, his huge stride taking him across the width of the atrium in just a few steps. Stark could already guess whom Dolph would pick to take with him. Dolph was a fierce soldier, but he was predictable and a little slow on the uptake. No matter; a blunt tool was more than sufficient for the job at hand.

Chapter 12

"Whoa, hold on a minute," said Mary. "What do you mean, 'lying'?"

They had barely begun their drive from the senator's house back toward Manhattan before Mary let loose a torrent of questions. Leopold had yet to provide a satisfactory answer, and Mary wasn't trying to hide her irritation.

"Spit it out then," she pressed. "We can't go round accusing senators of lying without any evidence!"

"I'm not going to accuse him of anything," Leopold replied calmly, turning in his seat to face her. "I know he's lying, which will help us figure this whole mess out. I'm not saying I know what the truth is. Yet."

Jerome turned onto the main road back to the city and put his foot down. The SUV reached cruising speed quickly, the sound of the engine and the wind noise coming through from the gaps in the crumpled chassis forcing Mary to raise her voice.

"Fine. Then at least tell me why you're so convinced he wasn't being honest," Mary demanded.

Leopold sighed. He had hoped that Mary would simply trust his judgment, but he supposed he was far too used to Jerome's unquestioning loyalty.

"First of all," he began, "picture what the senator was wearing."

"Yes, I remember," said Mary. "He had been up all night, still dressed in the same clothes he was wearing the day before."

"That was the intended effect," the consultant explained, "though his shirt was a creased mess, it was clean on that morning – I could smell the laundry detergent. A man doesn't wear the same shirt for more than twenty-four hours and still smell like he's just put on freshly washed clothes."

Mary didn't look convinced.

"Add to that," Leopold continued, "his behavior throughout the visit. Take his drinking, for example. He poured himself a measure of scotch from a sealed bottle. Why wait until we'd arrived to start drinking? I didn't see any empty bottles or used glasses in the other parts of the house, and the scotch was the only bottle in the cabinet."

"So what?"

"So, he's either running out of booze, or he simply wants to be *seen* to be drinking. As though that will give him the appearance of a desperate man."

"I'm not buying it," said Mary.

"Why else would he only start drinking when we arrived, except to be sure we would be there to see it?"

"It seems like reasonable behavior to me," said Mary, "considering the circumstances."

"By itself I wouldn't have thought twice, but it was other things too. His bed was unmade, but he hadn't slept last night? A sloppy mistake."

"He's just distracted, that's all."

Leopold leaned in closer to the police sergeant, his voice becoming more animated. "Do you remember what he asked us to do, Mary?"

"Of course," she replied. "He asked us to find Christina."

"Think carefully. The senator's actual instructions to us were that we needed to find the *kidnapper*, not his daughter. He couldn't even bring himself to mention Christina's name. I'd bet my life Senator Logan knows exactly who the kidnapper is, but what I can't figure out is why he wouldn't tell us."

"If he's involved, why would he hire you?" asked Mary.

"He'll want to be seen doing the right thing. It's better to have someone like me – someone you're paying – working for you, rather than getting the FBI involved," said Leopold. "Unfortunately for him, he thinks I'm the kind of person who would allow himself to be controlled."

"Say you're right, and I'm not saying you are, but let's pretend what you're saying makes *any* sense – how do we get some answers? I'd like to avoid getting into any car chases, if I can help it."

"Oh, that's easy. We go find Christina and ask her a few questions," said Leopold, pulling the folded piece of paper out of his jacket pocket. "These two names are a good place to start looking."

"What if someone's tracking us? Those guys that ran you off the road probably aren't the only ones looking for you."

"We can do a sweep for any tracking units once we get into the city," said Leopold. "If we find anything, there shouldn't be any issues removing it. Anyone wanting to follow us is going to have to use a more old fashioned approach."

Chapter 13

Christina's eyelids flickered, letting in some of the dim light. She was sitting upright, that much she could tell, and the chair was cold and hard. She tried to stand up, but found she couldn't move. A quick glance confirmed she was tied to a chair with some kind of rope, unable to move her limbs or hands. The room where she was sat was warm and smelled of dust, as if it hadn't been used in quite some time.

She blinked hard several times and the room shifted slowly into focus as her eyes tried to make out familiar shapes in the gloom. A gray shadow moved in the corner. There was something else in the room with her.

"Are we awake?" asked the shadow.

Christina tried to speak but couldn't find the words. The shadow moved again, drawing nearer. She could make out a face now, and eyes flecked with silver, catching the little light available in the room.

"We're going to have some fun with you," said the shadow.

Christina felt a hand on her shoulder. The shadow caressed her bare skin with thick, rough palms, gently stroking her neck and arms. She wanted to be sick.

Whatever drugs were in her system were playing tricks on her mind. This wasn't happening.

Then Christina saw the knife and screamed.

CHAPTER 14

Jerome pulled the SUV over to the curb on West 114th and turned off the engine. After a cursory sweep of the vehicle's exterior, the bodyguard located a small black box fixed to the inside of one of the wheel arches. He tossed the device into a nearby trash can and kneeled down to get a better view of the undercarriage. Satisfied, he gave the all clear and gestured the others out of the car.

Columbia University's enormous Butler Library backed onto the street, which was lined with rows of brick-fronted apartment buildings owned by the University Trust. The street was adorned with flags, hanging haphazardly from the many bookstores and apartment blocks that loomed overhead, but the wind hadn't yet picked up enough to rouse them. Jerome fed a handful of change into the parking meter, and the three of them made toward a set of tall black gates that opened onto the rear entrance path to the University's Morningside campus.

It was only just midday and the sun was out in full, along with what seemed like the entire university student body. The path opened out onto an enormous courtyard, with Butler Library at the closest end and the Low Memorial Library at the farthest. In between the two buildings was an expansive grassy area signposted as South Lawn, which was intersected with pathways leading up to the steps of the library, where a crowd of students shuffled around looking for their parents following the graduation ceremony earlier in the day. Hundreds of others were either walking through the campus or were sitting on the grass reading, laughing, or playing Frisbee. Leopold led the way toward the Low Memorial Library steps at the far end of the lawns, where the University's administrative departments were housed, weaving in and out of the crowd.

"I ran a search on Stark," said Jerome, catching up to Leopold and holding out his cell phone. "There's an entry on here from several years ago that caught my eye."

"Ex-military?" asked the consultant.

"Yes, just like the senator said. Except this particular branch of the military only takes the best of the best. Stark was the leader of a black ops team stationed in the Middle East until five years ago."

"What happened?"

"Stark was discharged for engaging the enemy during a ceasefire," said Jerome. "Turns out nobody told him the war was over. His entire unit was rounded up and sent packing."

"Great, just what we need," said Leopold. "A team of super-soldiers with a grudge. Let's hope Stark's on our side."

"We'd know if he held a grudge against us," said Jerome, pointing to the screen. "Apparently, he flew into a rage after his commanding officer took the stand. Threatened to assault the man as he took his seat."

"Not a fan of authority figures?"

Jerome nodded and kept walking. The Low Library building loomed overhead, casting a shadow over the steps as the sun crept slowly overhead. The entrance was sheltered by ten towering columns, over fifty feet tall and made from gleaming white marble. Inside, the domed ceiling rose one hundred feet above the main hall, and the walls were lined with busts of notable Greek and Roman philosophers, who glared menacingly at the crowd of students going about their business below. Leopold led Jerome and Mary through to the back of the hall, blinking hard as his eyes slowly adjusted to the dim light.

"To find Christina," said Leopold, his voice echoing slightly, "we need to access the University's student records and track down where these classmates of hers live, so we can ask them a few questions."

"How can we get access?" said Mary.

"All I need to do is scan the area for the University's wifi network," said Leopold. "My cell phone can emit a radio frequency that will block all wireless transmissions within a fifty foot radius, cutting off access to anyone linked up to the network. Then, when we turn off the jammer, we can piggyback on another device as it tries to log back in."

"I have no idea what you just said," said Mary, "but I guess that means you can hack into the University's files?"

"Yes. But you make it sound so *simple*," said Leopold.

Mary smiled and shrugged. Leopold swiped the cell phone's screen to unlock it and proceeded to activate the program. Less than a minute later, the software connected to the University network, and Leopold ran a quick search of the student records for the names that Senator Logan had provided.

"They're not far," said Jerome, "living in university-owned accommodation on the corner of 114th and Broadway."

"Fantastic," said Mary. "Looks like we parked in the right spot."

CHAPTER 15

Stark was a patient man. He had completed tours in Afghanistan, Iraq, and countless other places where he and his team of highly trained soldiers could be best put to use. If the government needed delicate work carried out with zero exposure, Stark and his team were the number one choice. On the forty-seven missions he had commanded, Stark had always achieved his objectives and he was not about to break his winning streak now. The colonel didn't leave anything to chance and no detail, however small, ever escaped his attention. Dealing with high-profile clients was no exception to this rule.

Following several unscheduled visits to the house, Stark had advised the senator to make sure that a member of his team was present during all meetings, to ensure any security risks were properly managed. The senator had eventually agreed, on the condition that the colonel himself be present and that anything said during the meetings be treated in the strictest confidence. Stark didn't relish the idea of bugging every room in the house, so he had agreed and signed a nondisclosure form.

Today's meeting was with the three businessmen from Washington, one of several meetings they had held in the last week that Stark had been forced to endure. Standing quietly at the back of the richly-decorated room, the soldier thought back with fondness to his days in combat. Hopefully, his chance would come again soon.

"Senator, I'm sure you can understand the situation we're in here," said one of the suits, a smug expression on his face.

"Why don't you spell it out for me?" replied Logan, his impatience almost tangible.

"It's the nature of politics, I'm afraid," the second suit chimed in. "We have to see some kind of commitment from you before we can do the same. You know how it is."

"If you mean financial commitment, I am working on a package right now. I had aimed to have a proposal for you by today, but I'm afraid we've run into an unforeseen roadblock. Nothing to worry about, I assure you. I'll have something solid for you by tomorrow."

"Good, good," said suit number three, slapping his palm across the senator's shoulder. "I'm glad we can stay friends."

The colonel watched the old politician recoil as though something disgusting had brushed up against him, but the three suits didn't seem to notice. Stark would have broken the man's wrist. They would have noticed that.

"So, to confirm: When I provide the initial capital, your organization will provide the rest of the sum required?" asked the senator.

"As we discussed, yes," said suit number one. "My organization can provide up to two hundred million, provided you can meet your side of the deal," he added.

"You'll have the details soon," said Logan.

"Good. Now, on to the good part," said suit number three, relaxing into the chair and putting his hands behind his head. "We need to start thinking about your campaign. It's election year, so concentrate on keeping your place in the senate for now. Once you're confirmed for another term, we'll start putting the wheels in motion."

"And what will that involve?" asked the senator.

"The key to any successful run for office is to get the swing voters on your side early. We can start looking at that now. By the time the election results are in this year, we'll already know our plan of attack. We can take care of mapping out the next six years in their entirety and get everything in place early. We just need your commitment."

"I've already said you'll have it. I'd like to hear some specifics of what your organization can guarantee."

"There are never guarantees in politics, Senator," said suit number two, leaning forward. "You of all people should know that. What we can provide, in exchange for certain… shall we say, *policy concessions*, is a shot at the title. And that's more than anyone else can count on, so we need to be sure we're backing the right man."

"You have my word," said the senator, briskly. "And that's all I can give for now. You'll hear from my assistant this afternoon. Now, gentlemen, is there anything else you would like to discuss?"

"We'll speak again this afternoon, I think," said suit number one, getting up and holding out his hand. "We'll say goodbye for now."

Logan remained seated and shook suit number one's hand. The other two nodded politely, and the three men left the room and walked into the hallway, where Viktor was waiting to show them out. Stark wanted to make sure their guests weren't left alone during their visit, not even for a second. Viktor shut the door softly behind them.

"Make sure that the telephone systems are operational by lunch time," said the senator. "Your encryption software is wreaking havoc with the lines, and I need to speak to the insurance company and my bank in Zurich urgently."

"Yes, sir," said Stark.

The senator left the room. The colonel stood alone in the plush study and noted with disgust that the value of the furniture alone would be enough to feed a large family for several months, at least. Stark understood that power and money went hand in hand. He understood that the link between politics and wealth was as old as time itself, and he knew that his country's fate was decided by the privileged few. But he didn't have to like it.

Today's America was different. In earlier times the country had fought itself free of tyranny and had forged an empire that now spanned the entire globe. Perhaps not an empire in the traditional sense, but an empire of economics and political power that affected the lives of more than seven billion people. Today's America was weak in comparison, left frail by the disease of corruption that went all the way to the White House. Crippled by the endless greed that had sucked the soul out of this once-great nation. A nation that millions of men had died fighting to protect.

The battle-worn soldier recalled the days when distinguishing between good and evil was a lot simpler. During his combat days, Stark would simply follow orders and trust that his superiors were on the right side. Now, in his civilian life, he found those lines had become blurred, and evil was no longer wearing armor and carrying a rifle, it was dressed in an expensive suit, armed with a bright smile, and carrying a *Mont Blanc* pen.

Stark made his way back to the entrance hall, pausing as he passed the photograph of the senator and the president shaking hands at the birthday party. Two men, smiling and laughing in the knowledge they were safe and secure, unaware of the people who had suffered and died to protect their way of life.

The tiny earpiece nestled in Stark's ear canal crackled, and Dolph's voice came on the line. The colonel listened to the report with growing concern and adjusted his orders accordingly. It wouldn't be long before Blake and his friends discovered what the senator had done. The next phase of the plan would need to be moved up a little.

Chapter 16

Leopold, Mary, and Jerome stood outside the Columbia halls of residence, fumbling with a folded paper map of Manhattan and trying to look like tourists. A heaving crowd pushed past them, largely uninterested. Every now and then the towering bodyguard would catch the attention of the more curious passers-by, but his cold stare ensured they didn't linger. Most of the people on the streets were dressed in business suits, many carrying briefcases and wearing thin overcoats. Despite the unseasonal warmth, the threat of sudden rain showers kept the summer wardrobes at bay. One particular figure, dressed unusually in a long coat and brimmed hat, passed close by, but kept his eyes down and his hands in his pockets. A few students passed by carrying stacks of heavy text books, chatting animatedly.

Though this was an upmarket part of town, there was still no shortage of hustle and the smell of warm bodies mingled with the whoosh of musty metal-tinged air rising up from the subway. The unseasonal heat and the thick humidity of the city were beginning to feel oppressive, as though there were a constant weight pressing in from all sides, prickling the skin.

Leopold dabbed at his brow with a handkerchief and wished they were indoors taking advantage of the air conditioning.

"Looks like we've got our chance," said Jerome, pointing at the small group of students heading toward the locked doors that led into the halls.

The three of them slipped through the doors as they swung closed and crossed the lobby to the elevators where they rode to the thirteenth floor. The corridors were busy as dozens of students returned to their dorm rooms to grab their books for the afternoon classes before going for lunch. Many were standing in the hallway, curiously eyeing the strangers as they walked down the corridor to room 1340, which nestled at the farthest end of one of the lesser-populated areas.

When they reached the room, Jerome tapped lightly on the door, which opened quickly to reveal the grinning face of a slim, blonde student, her hair hanging casually at shoulder length and her blue eyes framed by expensive-looking glasses. She wore a preppy halter top in navy blue with white polka dots, skinny jeans, and a pair of dark heels. Her expression was paused, as though she had been expecting someone else. With one hand resting on a tilted hip, she looked like a walking J.Crew commercial. Behind her, the girl's roommate looked up from her bed and shot the trio a quizzical look. She looked and dressed much the same, though was maybe ten or eleven pounds heavier, and didn't pretend to be pleased to see them.

"Hi," said the slim blonde. She had aimed the question at Jerome, but her eyes flickered over to Leopold when she didn't receive a response.

"Hi," said Leopold, "I wonder if you could help us. We're looking for Christina Logan. I understand that you girls know her pretty well."

The slim blonde raised her free hand up to the door frame and looked back at her roommate, who shrugged lazily.

"What's this about?" she asked, shifting her weight uncomfortably.

Leopold glanced at Mary and flicked his eyes in the direction of the girl. Mary took the hint.

"We're friends of Christina's dad," Mary said softly. "There's nothing to worry about. We just know that Christina hasn't been around for a few days, and her dad's really worried. Would it be okay if we came inside and asked you some questions?"

The girl looked back at her roommate again. "Sure, I guess."

"Thank you. My name's Mary," she held out a hand.

"Isabelle," said the slim blonde, taking her outstretched palm, "and this is Beth." Isabelle thumbed toward her roommate.

"It's nice to meet you," said Mary, stepping through into the dorm room.

Once the police sergeant had crossed over from the hallway, Jerome and Leopold followed, quietly closing the door behind them. The dorm room itself was of modest size, with two single beds separated by a nightstand. The room had two desks, upon which sat an array of jumbled textbooks, handwritten notes, and stuffed animals. Both girls had laptops flipped open on the beds; Isabelle's was dimmed and Beth was using hers to check email. Jerome and Leopold stood near the door, not quite sure what to do with themselves, as Mary took a seat on the empty bed and motioned for Isabelle to sit down next to her.

"When's the last time you remember seeing Christina?" asked Mary.

"Monday, I think," said Isabelle.

"Okay, think back. What were you girls doing last time you were together?"

"We were at a coffee place around the corner, talking about this week's study group session and what time we were gonna go over there."

"And you three were going over there together?" asked the sergeant.

"Yeah. Christina said she'd meet us there around eight-thirty," said Isabelle. "Then she left and we haven't seen her since. She said she was going over to meet this guy she's been seeing."

"Belle!" Beth slapped the lid of her laptop closed and glared at Isabelle.

Isabelle looked nervously at Mary.

"Fine, tell her," Beth shrugged, turning back to her computer.

"Don't tell her dad," said Isabelle. "He'd kill her. The guy she's seeing isn't exactly someone her dad would *approve of*. He's not a nice guy."

"What do you mean?" pressed Mary.

"Well, I never saw it happen, but I'd see Christina with bruises on her arms and legs. She'd say she fell, or that she'd been knocked over during hockey practice, but it never felt right. This guy's a real piece of work. I'm pretty sure he's got a record."

Mary nodded in support. "What's this guy's name?"

"Hank. I don't know his last name. Christina would just vanish for days and then say she was just staying with him at his place off campus. I'll bet that's where she is. Just don't say anything to her dad, please," said Isabelle.

"Don't worry," said Mary, "we're just trying to find out where she is. We don't want to get her into any trouble."

"You're probably too late for that," said Beth, sitting up to face the police sergeant. "Christina's blind to this guy. She'd do anything for him. She's completely in love and there's no talking to her. It doesn't matter how much of a bastard he can be, or how he treats her. She always defends him and says it's her fault. Makes me fucking sick. This is the guy."

Beth scribbled Hank's address down on a piece of scrap paper and handed it to Mary. "Here's a picture," she said, holding up her phone. "Don't tell him we sent you."

"Thanks for talking to me," said Mary. "We'll make sure Christina gets home safe."

She stood up and walked over to the door, nodding at the two girls reassuringly. Jerome and Leopold followed her out the door, and they rode the elevator back down to the lobby together.

"That was good work," said Leopold, as they walked out onto the street. "You really connected with those girls. Got us just the lead we needed."

"You really think the boyfriend has anything to do with this?" asked Mary, as the elevator opened up to the entrance hall with a subdued chime.

"It's a good place to start. Besides, if he's not the one pulling the strings, he should at least be able to tell us where Christina went after she met up with him."

"I don't like the sound of this guy," said Mary, her expression hardening. "I don't know if I'm going be able to hold myself back if it turns out he's beating her."

"I wouldn't worry about that," said Leopold. "I'd be more concerned about what Jerome might do."

Chapter 17

It had been easy enough to gain access to Hank's building. As Leopold had predicted, they were immediately buzzed in once Jerome had informed a neighbor they were there to check the gas lines, following the report of a leak. The tenant they spoke to simply told them to let themselves out when they had finished.

The bodyguard led the way as they climbed the stairs to Hank's seventh-floor apartment. The only other movement in the building was on the third floor, where a team of decorators was making renovations. The stairwell smelled of new paint, and judging by the mess the decorators had left, it looked like each apartment was being given a full revamp. They reached Hank's door and Jerome knocked heavily. There was no answer, so he tried the handle.

"Deadbolts."

"Do the honors, Jerome," said Leopold, gesturing for Mary to stand behind him.

The huge bodyguard took a couple of big steps backward, lowered his shoulder, and charged. The door frame splintered as the force of his body ripped out the hinges and bolts, scattering pieces of wood all over the floor. Jerome stepped inside, kicking the debris to one side.

Hank's apartment was small and modestly furnished. The doorway opened into the living area, which also included a small kitchenette. To the right was a short hallway that led through to a cramped bedroom and a bathroom. The apartment had been recently decorated with a new coat of magnolia paint, except for the hallway, which was still exposed drywall. Overall, the apartment was meticulously arranged and scrubbed clean, with nothing out of place. Nothing except for the dead body that was slumped up against the wall.

"No one's here; place is deserted," said Jerome, his hand still resting on his firearm as he returned from checking the other rooms.

Leopold knelt by the body. The dead man was wearing casual clothes, had short brown hair and was decorated with numerous ear piercings and tattoos. Leopold noticed tiny red marks on the inside of his elbow, probably from drug use. The dead man's left wrist had been slashed, leaving a gash that ran half the length of his forearm. Thick, dark blood had pooled around his arms and legs, staining the carpet where he sat. He held a serrated knife in his right hand, the blade flecked with dried blood.

Mary knelt down next to Leopold and fished the man's wallet from inside his back pocket, tilting the body slightly to allow her access.

"This is Hank," said the sergeant, examining the driver's licence and getting back up on her feet.

Leopold leaned in closer and examined the wound. Hank's injuries appeared to have been caused by the serrated blade he was holding, judging by the tears in the flesh surrounding the deep gash on his arm. There were no other signs of injury on the body, although a full autopsy would be required to know for sure.

"Whoever did this took their time," said the consultant, squinting closer at the deep cut. "The wound is very convincing."

"What do you mean?" asked Mary, getting to her feet.

"Hank committing suicide is too great a coincidence, considering everything that's happened," said the consultant, frowning.

"Sure, I can buy that. But we'll need more than circumstantial evidence to prove murder."

"And there's the rub. Whoever is leaving the trail of bodies is making them look just enough like suicides to give a jury enough reasonable doubt to throw out a murder charge."

"There must be some evidence we can use.".

"The blood pooling around Hank's body is a little darker than I would have expected," said Leopold, pointing to the stains on the carpet. "This happens when the heart isn't pumping enough oxygen into the blood, and is usually caused when something constricts the oxygen supply."

"Someone strangled him?" asked Jerome, from across the room.

"Not likely," replied Leopold, "otherwise we'd see bruising around the neck. However, I do think his airways were constricted prior to death. Mostly likely something inserted into the wind pipe, which would be much harder to detect during an autopsy."

"Why not just let him choke?" asked Mary.

"The point is to make it look like a suicide. People don't usually dispatch themselves by sticking foreign objects into their windpipes, and if Hank had died prior to the wrists being cut we'd be able to tell. Judging by the lack of color around his face and lips, I'm certain it's the blood loss that killed him."

"So the killer stopped Hank breathing just long enough for him to pass out?" asked the police sergeant.

"Yes. Cutting off his oxygen for long enough beforehand would have made it far easier to arrange Hank in this position. If he'd struggled, the killer might not have been able to be so convincing."

"Not convincing enough for you. But I'd imagine it's convincing enough for a jury," said Mary. "Just one question: How did the killer get out? The door was locked from the inside when we arrived."

"Check the windows," said Leopold.

Jerome unlatched the living room window, which opened just enough to fit his forearm through.

"The windows don't open all the way," he remarked. "No chance anyone could have fit their whole body through, even if they did ignore the fifty-foot drop."

Leopold took a few minutes to examine the rest of the apartment. The tiny kitchen was littered with unopened mail that had been left on the countertop, and there was a strong smell of decomposing food coming from underneath the sink. He pulled open one of the cupboard doors and recoiled as the smell from the open garbage can hit his nose and he quickly shut the door again. He turned to leave, but noticed a letter lying open on top of the pile of junk mail. He picked it up and studied it carefully.

"Found anything?" asked Mary.

"Just a bank statement," said Leopold. "Nothing unusual. We can use the account reference to check for any irregularities. Should save us getting a warrant, at least."

Mary walked over and examined the piece of paper in the consultant's hand.

"You can't just hack in to someone's private account."

"Actually, I can," said Leopold, punching Hank's details into his cell phone. "I have a contact who can look into this sort of thing. I'll send everything over. Shouldn't take long."

He hit the send button, ignoring the sergeant's protestations, and turned his attention back to Hank's body.

"We need to keep looking," said Mary. "There must be something here that can explain what happened that doesn't involve us breaking about fifty federal laws."

"We can start with the laptop in the bedroom," said Jerome. "There's probably something on the hard drive we can use."

The bodyguard led the way into the bedroom and pointed out the laptop, shoved into a corner of the bed and partially obscured by the pillows. The bedding and furniture was old, but the room itself had been recently redecorated, like the rest of the apartment. Leopold picked up the laptop and turned it on, taking a seat on the bed. The others peered in over his shoulder.

"This is definitely Christina's laptop," said Leopold, "judging by the number of college papers on here. Looks like she's left her email open."

He scrolled through the emails and noticed that among the unread messages, one sender kept jumping out.

"Cupid," said the consultant, jabbing the screen with his index finger.

"Who?" said Mary.

"Christina has received at least a dozen emails from someone calling himself 'Cupid.' Looks like an anonymous sender."

He opened up the latest message for them all to see. The message read:

I know what you did and I'm going to tell. You can't hide from me any more. You're going to get what's coming to you.

Chapter 18

Senator Logan sat at the desk in his bedroom, staring intently at the bank of slim computer monitors in front of him. Stark couldn't quite make out what the text read from where he was standing in the doorway, but it looked like a list of banking transactions

"You asked to see me sir?" said the colonel, knocking softly on the open door.

"Yes, I need an update on Blake," said Logan, turning off the monitors.

"They found Hank, sir. He's dead."

The senator turned his desk chair to face his chief security officer, a look of deep concern on his face. "This is very disturbing news," he said. "Do they know what happened?"

"My team's surveillance equipment picked up most of their conversation. Blake is saying Hank was murdered. They've also found a lead on Christina's computer; it appears that someone was sending her threatening emails."

"Threatening what?"

"We don't know, sir. But we understand they're going to try and track down the computer the messages were sent from."

"Good," said the senator. "Keep an eye on them. If they find anything, let me know immediately. I can't afford any more delays."

Stark nodded, and the senator turned back to his monitors, signaling the end of the conversation. The colonel left the room and closed the door behind him. He paced across the thick carpet and entered one of the empty guest bedrooms, a large room with an immaculately prepared king-sized bed against the far wall. Facing the fireplace on the opposite wall were two leather armchairs, arranged either side of a mahogany coffee table. Satisfied he couldn't be overheard, Stark took a seat and patched his comms system through to Dolph's earpiece.

"Your orders, sir?" said the blond.

"Keep an eye on Blake and don't underestimate his bodyguard."

"Yes, sir. Have the senator's plans changed?"

"No, we're still on track."

"And if Blake finds anything?"

"If the plan is compromised, make sure you use the German. He's in the vicinity if we need him. Don't take any risks. We can't have this traced back to us."

Stark turned off his earpiece. Thanks to Blake's bodyguard, it would be almost impossible to follow them much further without being spotted, and Dolph would have to drop back and risk losing them in the crowd. Without an audio link, it would be difficult to keep track of Blake's progress. No matter; in a few hours the game would be over. And Stark always won.

Chapter 19

"So how do we find Cupid?" asked Mary. "I can think of a few questions I'd like to ask this guy."

"We'll start with an email trace," said Leopold. "Jerome has a contract in place with the same company that handles data sniffing for the CIA, so this should be a piece of cake. I just need to log in to their database and run the program."

He isolated the email's source code and opened the text in the web browser. Accessing the online database, he copied in the code and hit *confirm* once he had finished. Less than a minute later, he received an email with a file attachment.

"Okay, let's open it up," said Leopold, downloading the file.

The computer screen showed a two-dimensional map of Manhattan, with a pulsing red dot indicating the origin of the email and a green dot showing their current location. The message had been sent from just a couple of miles away. He zoomed in to street level.

"That's strange," said Leopold.

"What is it?" asked Mary

"According to the tracer, the email originated from a computer somewhere on the Columbia campus, but according to the maps, there are no buildings within at least a hundred feet of its location."

"So maybe the tracer is a little inaccurate. Or maybe someone just used a laptop. At least we know someone at the University has been threatening Christina."

"Actually, this software is cutting edge and accurate to within three feet," said Leopold, scrolling through a long text file that had accompanied the tracer results. "According to the data here, the email was sent from a machine hooked up to a hard line, so it couldn't have been a laptop or cell phone. It would have to be a computer linked up to the University's own physical network via cable."

"Wouldn't a machine like that be inside?" asked Mary. "There's no buildings there."

"That's the problem with two dimensional maps," said the consultant, frowning. "They can't tell you anything about elevation. The computer we're looking for must be underground. The University keeps its storage and archive rooms beneath the main campus, and plenty of areas will have been sealed off over time. We just need to get down there and take a look."

"How do we get in?" asked Mary. "Most of the campus is closed to the public."

"Thankfully, I'm not a member of the general public. According to rumor, Columbia has a series of underground tunnels that connect most of these rooms together," said Leopold, drawing a line on the map with his finger. "If we can get into the secured areas of the University, we can use the tunnels to get around unnoticed. Do you think you can turn on the charm if we run into security?"

"Of course," Mary smiled, and batted her eyelids to emphasize her point.

Leopold smiled back. "Good. Let's get moving, before Cupid works out we've accessed his machine and makes a run for it."

"What about the other evidence? We should catalogue it and keep it secured."

"Spoken like a true police officer. It'll still be here later. Right now we have to get hold of Cupid before he slips away for good. You need to put in the call to the precinct and have someone you trust come down here and seal off the apartment."

"No problem," said Mary, pulling out her cell phone.

"And make sure they don't *touch* anything," said Leopold. "I've got enough to worry about without finding doughnut powder over all the forensic evidence."

Mary scowled and made the call.

Chapter 20

Leopold was excited. He'd heard many rumours about the tunnels under Columbia and had read extensively on the subject, although he had never had the chance to explore them personally. Until now. The oldest tunnels predated the existence of the University campus, when Morningside Heights was home to the Bloomingdale Insane Asylum. Since the University was granted permission to block itself off from the main thoroughfares, the tunnels had fallen largely into disuse, although Leopold knew that a small minority of students still devoted much of their energy to exploring the now-forbidden underground network.

Leopold, Mary, and Jerome arrived at the Columbia University campus just after lunch, as the crowds of students began to disperse. The consultant once again accessed the University's wireless network through his cell phone and ran a search as he led them back toward the Low Memorial Library.

"According to records, the first cabled network with Internet access was installed in the basement of Pupin Hall during the early nineties," said Leopold.

"Since then, the whole area was closed off, so that's a good place to start looking."

"Won't they have sealed off the basement from the tunnel entrance as well?" asked Mary.

"We'll have to hope not. Most of the tunnels are unmapped and potentially unstable, so carrying out any construction work down there would be a bad idea. My guess is they just locked up the classrooms and forgot about the place."

"You're making this sound like a really great idea, Leopold," said Mary. "How do we know this particular tunnel even exists?"

"We don't. But we have to at least assume some entrance exists; otherwise how would Cupid have access? We need to find someone who can get us into the tunnels and guide us through to the basement at Pupin."

"Where do we find someone like that?"

"I can make some calls," said Jerome "I know a good place to start looking."

The bodyguard dropped behind, talking quickly into his cell phone. The three of them made their way across the courtyard toward the Business School, an ugly stone-fronted building that loomed high over an otherwise pleasant garden area to the rear of the Low Library rotunda. The area was mostly deserted, despite the pleasant early afternoon sun, as most people had gone back inside for afternoon classes.

"Looks like I've found us a lead," said Jerome, "a guy by the name of Renard who runs unofficial tours of the Columbia tunnels. Apparently he's a former student and lives pretty close by."

"Did you get a telephone number?" asked Leopold.

"Yes, I'll give him a call now."

"Good. Ask him to meet us here at the Uris Hall Business School as soon as possible, and tell him we can pay cash."

Jerome dialed the number and waited for the call to go though. A few moments later, he hung up the phone and gave a thumbs-up.

"He'll be here in thirty minutes."

"Good. In the meantime, I've had some more information sent through about Hank," said Leopold, pulling out his own cell phone and scrolling through his long list of emails. "I got a hit on the bank account records we found. My contact sent through a summary of transactions for the last twelve months. Nothing out of the ordinary until just a few weeks ago."

"Let me guess," said Mary. "An unusually large cash deposit?"

"Correct. Twenty thousand dollars, to be precise. Paid to him in one instalment by a company called Greenway Investments."

"Greenway? Never heard of them."

"Neither had my contact. He tried to find some data, but all he could track down was a registered business address in The Bahamas."

"That's it?" asked Mary.

"For now. He's going to keep digging, but it sounds like a phantom to me. A business entity set up for the sole purpose of hiding money."

"Looks like we've hit a road block on this one."

"Not necessarily," said Leopold, punching a text message into his cell as he spoke. "It at least tells us something useful."

"And that is?"

Leopold slipped the smart phone back into his jacket pocket and looked Mary in the eye. "It tells us whoever made that payment didn't want to be found."

Chapter 21

Christina wanted to move, but her body wouldn't respond. The room hung hazily in front of her disjointed eyes, a blur of gray and white. There had been a bright light. There had been a man with silver eyes, and then there had been pain. But Christina couldn't remember why.

She remembered that the pain would stop when the kind man came in. The man with the silver eyes was afraid of him. The kind man had told her everything would be all right and had given her something to make the pain go away.

She forced her lazy eyes to focus and she saw the knife again. Cutting her flesh. Sliding the skin and muscle apart like butter. Christina smiled. All just a dream, floating through her mind like a wayward cloud.

The kind man would close up the wounds with silk, and he would smile when she didn't make a sound. She liked making him happy. He kept the man with silver eyes away when he was happy.

When he wasn't happy, she didn't get to dream anymore.

Chapter 22

Jerome caught Leopold's attention and motioned toward the small, dark silhouette approaching from the distance across South Lawn. As the figure grew closer Leopold could make out a short man dressed in crumpled clothes with unkempt and curly hair, a nervous and worried expression on his face. The man glanced about him and pulled up the collar on his jacket to obscure the bottom half of his face. The shabby figure approached and held out his hand.

"You the ones who called?" he said, his voice low.

"Who are you?" asked Jerome, ignoring the hand stretched out in front of him.

"Renard, of course. You can call me Albert."

"So now we know exactly who you are and why you're here. Rookie move. How do you know what we'd do with that information?" demanded the bodyguard.

Albert looked away sheepishly and thrust his hands into his pockets.

"Look," he said, "I'm a busy guy. What do you guys need?"

"We want a tour of the tunnels," said Leopold, "especially the network that runs underneath Pupin."

"What's so special about Pupin?"

"We're history nuts," the consultant lied. "Pupin used to be the headquarters for some top-secret weapons research during the second world war. We heard there might be some of the original equipment sealed in the basement and we want to go take a look. Your name came up as a guy who might be able to help."

"No chance you're getting into Pupin," said Albert. "The lower floors were locked up years ago. No one gets in."

"So I guess you won't be wanting the two thousand dollars, then?" Leopold pulled a roll of hundred dollar bills out of his pocket and held them up.

Albert paused for a few moments, then glanced quickly from side to side and took the roll of notes.

"Okay, okay," he sighed, "there *might* be a way in. Only hypothetical, mind you. I still keep in touch with some of the students here that continue the work I started before I got kicked out. There was talk of a possible way through, but it's not something I've had chance to check out. It could be a dead end."

"We'll risk it," said Leopold. "Where do we start?"

"The easiest access point is inside here." Their tour guide pointed toward Uris Hall. "As long as we can get into the building, we should be able to access the tunnels. Then we can follow the network through to the area underneath Pupin, and hopefully get lucky."

"Why can't we just go in through Pupin Hall?" asked Mary. "I'm not totally sold on the idea of crawling through a bunch of tunnels just for the sake of it."

"It wouldn't work," said Albert. "The first five stories of Pupin are actually underneath where we're standing now, and they sealed off all the internal routes down to the lower levels years ago. Believe me, I tried to get in that way."

"You've tried to get in before?" asked Mary.

"Yeah, of course. I actually came close once, but I was caught before I got a chance to finish mapping the tunnels in that area, and all my notes got taken. Since I got kicked out, I've been relying on my sources inside the University to provide updates on new routes, as well as making the occasional expedition myself."

"Okay, fine, but if these shoes get ruined I'm coming after you," said the police sergeant, eying Leopold.

The consultant grinned and motioned for Albert to lead the way. The four of them headed toward the big double doors of Uris Hall.

"Getting in is surprisingly easy," said the tour guide eagerly, "when they forget to erase your pass card from the security systems."

Albert swiped his card across the magnetic reader and the lock disengaged. He held the door open and Jerome, Leopold, and Mary stepped through into the lobby. The interior of the building was pristine, with polished floors stretching out in all directions before branching into corridors that snaked out into the distance. The walls were largely bare, with a few photographs of notable alumni hanging at sparse intervals along the width of the atrium. Other than the four intruders, the building appeared to be entirely deserted.

"We've got about twenty minutes before the next set of classes begin and everyone moves out into the corridors," said Albert. "Which should be just enough time to get down to the tunnel entrance in the basement."

The tour guide took the lead and motioned for the others to follow him toward one of the corridors. The four of them passed through a series of double doors and several other deserted corridors before finding themselves an open area that contained a few easy chairs, a vending machine and a large poster board covered in sign-up sheets, advertisements and lists of classrooms. To the rear was a door that read *Private: University Staff Only*.

"That door leads through to the lower levels and the basement, where the tunnels start," said Albert. "It's usually unlocked during the day, so we shouldn't have too much of an issue getting down there. We just have to keep an eye out for the security guards doing their rotation."

He reached for the door handle and pulled, but the door didn't budge. He rattled the door several times before giving up.

"Shit!" cursed Albert, under his breath. "The only other way through is at the other side of the building, and there's currently a packed lecture hall in the way."

"Okay, so we just wait until the class finishes and slip in through the crowd," said Mary.

"That's not gonna work," said the tour guide. "I've spent a lot of time plotting the routes that the security guards take, and we've only got a few minutes before they start sweeping the areas near the tunnels. They like to make sure students don't disappear down there in between classes."

"Well, it's not like we can force our way in," said Leopold. "The noise would give us away."

"Relax," said Jerome, patting his employer on the shoulder with a heavy palm. "You're all acting as though this is my first covert mission."

The bodyguard strode across to the other side of the room, stopping next to the fire alarm. Without saying a word he slammed his fist against the thin glass, filling the building with the piercing sound of alarm bells. Within seconds, Leopold could hear chairs scraping against the floor and doors being flung open as hundreds of students abandoned their classes and made their way to the fire exits.

Without wasting any time, Jerome charged, using the noise and distraction to mask the sound of the door breaking as his body collided with it. He focused the impact on the area near the handle, causing the lock to break but ensuring that the door didn't come off its hinges. Jerome hurried the others through and quickly closed the door behind them, just as the first of many students rounded the corner.

Albert breathed a sigh of relief and then turned to face Leopold, a quizzical look on his face. "You guys aren't tourists, are you?"

Chapter 23

The gloss and air conditioning of the public corridors gave way to damp air and bare concrete as Albert, Leopold, Jerome, and Mary made their way to the basement. The dim passageways that led through the older parts of the building were lined with exposed pipes and dim light bulbs that hung loosely from the ceiling. The rumble of HVAC units and the hiss of steam accompanied their footsteps, punctuated every now and again by the whizz and crackle of old circuit breaker boxes.

"It's not much further," said Albert, turning his head as he walked. "We should hurry, just in case they decide to run a security sweep down here."

"Why would they do that?" asked Mary.

"They'll be wondering who pulled the fire alarm. They usually run a quick sweep in between classes anyway, so chances are they'll step up their timetable now," said the tour guide, facing front again as he quickened his pace.

"Let's make sure they don't find us then," said Leopold, leaning in close to Mary so that Albert couldn't hear. "Otherwise our chances of finding Cupid are shot to hell. It's only a matter of time before he works out we traced him."

"Then all he needs to do is wipe the hard drive, and we've lost all the evidence linking him to this," said the police sergeant, whispering.

"Exactly, and he'll be able to do that remotely within a matter of minutes of finding the tracer we ran. This is our only chance to find this guy and hopefully find Christina. The longer she's missing, the less likely we find her alive."

Albert led the group deeper into the lower levels of the building, stopping only to make sure everyone was still behind him. After several minutes, the group reached the end of a narrow passageway and found their way blocked by a heavy metal door. Jerome tried the handle without success.

"Heavy mag-lock," he said, pulling hard on the handle. "The door won't budge. Doesn't look like we're going to be able to bust our way through this one."

"Dammit," said Albert, "this door wasn't here last time I came down. They must have upgraded security since last time."

"Why would they have done that?" asked Leopold.

"Well, I may not have mentioned this, but the last time I came down to the tunnels for a visit wasn't exactly *uneventful*." Albert shuffled uncomfortably.

"Spit it out," said Jerome, taking a step closer to their guide.

"Okay, okay. One of the security guards found me down here, maybe a couple of months ago. Nearly caught me too, but I was too fast for him. That must be why they've installed this new door."

"Great, just great," said Leopold. "How are we going to get through?"

"We need a magnetic key-card," said the bodyguard. "I'm betting the security guards have them as standard."

"That's not going to help us much," said Mary.

"Wait a minute," said Leopold, placing his hand on the tour guide's shoulder. "Albert, when you ran into security last time, how many of them were down here?"

"Just the one."

"Did he radio for backup?"

"No, he just yelled and ran after me."

The consultant nodded. "I think I've got a plan. If we can swipe the guard's key card, we can get down here before he's even realized it's gone."

"It's risky," said Jerome. "If it turns out he's got a radio, or a buddy on patrol with him, they could close on us pretty quick, and we lose our only window."

"It doesn't look like we have much of a choice," said Mary. "We need to find this Cupid sicko as soon as possible, before anything else happens to Christina. We've already got one dead body."

"Agreed," said Leopold, "we don't have any other options here."

"Did you say dead body?" asked Albert, his voice shaking slightly. "So what's the plan?" asked Mary, ignoring the tour guide's question.

"I have an idea," said Leopold, turning to face the police sergeant. "But I'm going to need your help."

CHAPTER 24

Marty O'Donnell, a campus security guard from Long Island, watched the throng of business and economics students milling around outside Uris Hall enjoying the impromptu break in classes and the chance to enjoy some fresh air. Marty folded his arms and glared at the crowd, watching for any sign of trouble. He knew someone had pulled the fire alarm as a prank, and he was determined to find the culprit.

Marty stood a little over five foot six and weighed upwards of two hundred and twenty pounds, none of which was muscle. He wore a pale blue short-sleeved shirt and clip-on tie, with a nightstick and set of keys clipped loosely to his belt, which was a couple of notches too small for his considerable waistline. His physical appearance hadn't changed much since childhood, and Marty had developed a mean attitude as a way of coping with the inevitable bullying during high school. Now pushing forty, his attitude had only worsened, and he was itching for an opportunity to exercise some pent-up aggression.

He stared intently at the crowd and focused on a small group of students who had started playing Frisbee. Marty smiled. With the alarm bells still wailing behind him, he strode out toward the lawn and beckoned the students to come over.

"What do you think you're doing?" said Marty.

"Playing Frisbee. What's wrong with that?" said one of the students, a skinny kid with long hair.

"What's wrong is we're in the middle of a possible fire emergency, that's what's wrong," said the security guard, pointing his finger at the skinny kid. "Do you think if the building was on fire right now that playing Frisbee would be a good idea?"

"Yeah, but the building's *not* on fire," said the skinny kid.

"That's not the point, smartass," growled Marty. "It's my job to keep you idiots safe, and that means no goofing off when there's a fire alarm. You know what I see when I look at you? Trouble, that's what. And if it turns out someone pulled the fire alarm as a prank, you're the first person I'm coming for."

He snatched the Frisbee away, tucked it under his arm, and marched back to his vantage point just in front of the main doors and waited for the alarms to die down. After several minutes of continued racket, the alarms were showing no sign of shutting off and the noise grew even more distracting as a crescendo of sirens began to sound above the shrill clang of the alarm bells.

Marty was confused. The Uris alarm systems weren't rigged to contact the emergency services; they were too old-fashioned for that, and it was unlikely any of the students would have made the call. Most of them wouldn't care if the whole place burned down. He pushed these thoughts to the back of his mind as three fire trucks rolled up the campus lawns and stopped just behind the mass of students, tearing deep tracks in the manicured lawn. Marty groaned as he realized he was going to get the blame for the repair bill.

With a growl, the security guard stormed in the direction the fire trucks, pushing past the crowd of students who had all turned around to see what was going on. He shoved a couple of bewildered students to the side and collided with a particularly striking brown-haired woman, causing both of them to stagger backward. The young woman flashed an apologetic smile and pushed a strand of hair back behind her ear before glancing up at him.

"Sorry about that," she said, "I wasn't looking where I was going with all this commotion. I hope I didn't hurt you."

Marty grunted a response and waved her away. It wasn't often beautiful women spoke to him, especially those he nearly knocked over. Shrugging, he resumed his stride and walked up to the group of firefighters who had now spilled out onto the grass.

"What the hell are you doing?" Marty shouted over the noise at the firefighter he assumed was in charge.

"Stand back, sir, this area is currently posing a fire risk."

"What the hell do you mean? There's no fire here."

"We received a call a few minutes ago that there was a fire at Uris Hall, Morningside campus of Columbia University. Is this the address?"

"Well, yes."

"And are those fire alarm bells?"
"Yes. But -"
"Then please let us do our job, sir."

Marty fumed, but reluctantly stepped back as the fire captain directed his team to the main entrance of the building. The crowd of students parted as the firefighters passed through, each wearing a protective suit and breathing apparatus. Soon the firemen had disappeared into the building and Marty was left to keep the peace outside, a prospect that made him no less irritable than he already was.

He drew the standard-issue nightstick from the holster on his belt and flicked it toward the ground with a snap of his wrist, extending it to full length with a sharp click. He began to walk slowly through the crowd, tapping the end of the weapon against his free palm in a manner he hoped would prove menacing enough to stop anyone from causing any trouble or asking any questions. *So far, so good.*

After a few minutes, Marty absent-mindedly reached to his belt with his free hand and noticed his set of keys was missing.

Chapter 25

"Got it!"

Mary ran into the corridor at full speed, nearly colliding with Albert, stopped sharply in front of Leopold, and held up a white key card attached to a set of metal keys.

"Good work. Did he see you?"

"Unfortunately, yes. He was walking around with one hand on his keychain and I could see the card attached by a lanyard. The only chance was to divert his attention, so I walked right into him."

"Did he notice you take the keys?"

"No, I don't think so."

"Okay, but we still don't have too much time. He's going to notice the keys are missing any minute and track us down here."

They all set off back in the direction of the basement, with Jerome dragging Albert by his collar amid subdued protestations that he should be allowed to go home.

"Keep quiet and you'll get to go home a lot sooner," said the bodyguard. "You're not going anywhere until you've earned your two thousand dollars."

"Earned it? I've watched you guys break down doors, set off alarms, call out the fire department under false pretences, and to top it all off, there's at least one dead body nobody's telling me about. I'd say I've earned my money!"

Jerome glared at the tour guide and tightened his grip. Albert took the hint and kept quiet.

A few minutes later the four of them reached the lower-level passageways for the second time, and Leopold opened the heavy mag-locked door with a quick swipe of the stolen key card. The lock released with a muffled clunk and the door opened outwards to reveal an even darker, damper passageway beyond.

Mary groaned. "You definitely owe me a new pair of shoes."

"I'll get you two," replied Leopold.

The group marched in single file down the passageway, pausing only as gusts of steam sporadically erupted from cracks in the pipe work that ran along the walls at roughly head height. The tunnel was dimly lit by bare light bulbs that hung from the ceiling, humming quietly to themselves in the wet air. Leopold could just about see ten feet or so into the distance and led the way, followed by Mary, with Jerome dragging Albert at the rear, protesting in short, squeaky breaths about how he should never have left the house. The consultant held up a hand and indicated they should pause for a moment.

"Albert, what seems to be the problem?" Leopold asked, not unkindly.

Their tour guide paused before replying and tugged his sleeve out of Jerome's grasp, "I'm not going any further until you tell me what's going on."

The bodyguard scowled.

"No, he's right, Jerome. Leopold, you should tell him why he's here," said Mary.

"Okay, I'll tell you the truth if you think it'll make you feel better. Though I'm not convinced it will."

Leopold sighed and told Albert an edited version of everything that had happened, leaving out some of the more questionable details. As he spoke, the tour guide's eyes widened in horror, but by the time Leopold had finished the tunnels expert was grinning with excitement.

"Fantastic!" He was bouncing up and down. "A real-life tunnelers mystery! This is probably the most exciting thing to happen to me since, well, forever! Count me in!"

Leopold was a little surprised by his response, but glad he no longer needed Jerome to drag Albert along by the scruff of his neck. It certainly made getting around a lot easier. He invited their guide to join him at the head of the group.

"Can you tell where we are?" asked Leopold.

"It's hard to tell exactly," replied Albert, "but I'd say we're about fifty feet or so from Pupin Hall. If they haven't completely sealed off the basement, we should be pretty close to getting in."

"How will you know?"

"Oh, that's easy. The stonework down here is well over a hundred years old; any recent work to close off the tunnels would immediately be obvious from the stone itself. See here?" he ran his fingers along the wall. "The walls are extremely porous, through decades of damp and dripping water. The consistency is also completely different; modern materials use entirely different mixtures. I'll be able to tell straight away."

"And if they haven't tried sealing it off?"

"If it's anything like the others, we'll see the pipes branch off and disappear into the ceiling once we're under the building. Pupin has to get its gas and electricity from somewhere."

Leopold nodded. "Lead the way."

A few minutes later Albert pointed excitedly as the group rounded a corner, where the tightly knit pipe work forked out into a complex mess of interwoven steel and copper lines. Leopold traced the pipes with his finger and noticed where the larger gas line disappeared into the ceiling.

"We're here," he said, turning to the guide. "I suppose there should be some kind of hatch that allows access."

"Exactly. This part of the tunnel network was never designed to provide pedestrian access, unlike some of the more well-known areas. The only reason people would be down here would be to repair the pipes, so we're looking for a small hatch, nothing fancy. Should lead directly up into the lower classrooms."

Mary and Jerome began scanning the ceiling for an entry hatch, while Leopold and Albert went ahead in case there was evidence of a way in further along the tunnel.

"Found something!" the bodyguard's deep voice boomed through the narrow passageway.

Leopold and Albert rushed back to find him pointing up at the ceiling. The consultant followed Jerome's finger with his eyes and settled on an area of the ceiling where he could just make out a rusted metal panel, nestled in the damp stonework. The hatch was just large enough for a fully grown adult to squeeze through, and had no handle to keep it closed; instead there was a padlock securing the hatch to its frame. Leopold shot a sideways glance at Jerome.

"Don't worry, I've fit through tighter spaces," Jerome said, noticing his employer's quizzical look. "I'll just have to breathe in a little, that's all."

The bodyguard examined the security guard's keys that Mary had managed to snatch and found one that looked like it would fit the padlock. With a little effort, the stiff lock snapped open and he lowered the hatch door carefully, interlocking his fingers to provide a boost for the others as they climbed through. Jerome followed shortly afterwards, hoisting his heavy frame through the hatchway with a surprising lack of effort. The group stood in the dark basement, each looking around for a light switch.

"Found it!" Albert flicked on the power.

Leopold looked around the room as his eyes adjusted to the bright lights. The walls, once white, were a speckled mess of gray dust and cobwebs. Running the length of the room were long wooden benches where scientists and students must have once scribbled notes on the piles of now-disused notepads; newspaper clippings; and various manuscripts. In the center of the room were a series of thick countertops at hip height, each complete with gas lines for Bunsen burners. A multitude of cracked and dirty microscopes filled up any empty spaces.

"Wow, this place is even better than I expected," said Albert, glancing around the room with growing excitement. "I should have come down here years ago."

"We don't have time for sightseeing," said Mary. "We need to find that computer and track down Cupid. It's only a matter of time before we lose this lead."

"Agreed," said Leopold. "Let's get moving. We're looking for a storage room, so we can ignore any of the classrooms down here. That should narrow it down considerably. Follow me."

He led the others out of the dusty laboratory and into the hallway, which was long and thin, with a number of wooden doors on each side. At the end of the hallway, the room split out into a narrow corridor that appeared to run the perimeter of the building. After a few minutes they found a heavy wooden door at the end of the corridor, about halfway around. Leopold stepped forward.

"This is the one. See where the handle has been used recently?"

The consultant pointed at oily marks that had tarnished the brass handle, then opened the door and stepped inside. Turning on the light, he smiled as he saw what waited for them inside. The room looked like it used to be an office, although now the dust and decay had rendered it useless. On top of the grimy desk in the center of the room stood an ancient computer monitor, taking up most of the space. Leopold strode over and found a keyboard and mouse hooked up to a battered desktop computer that was nestled underneath the desk. He tapped the keyboard and the monitor flickered to life, displaying simple green text on a black background asking for a recipient's email address. The cursor blinked impatiently.

"This shouldn't take too long," said Leopold, typing feverishly. "I just need to access the root logs for the system and find the exact time this machine was last used."

"And that will give us Cupid?" asked Mary.

"Not directly. But it will give us the exact date and time the last email to Christina was sent, which we can cross-reference with the security logs to find out who was nearby at the time."

"Clever," said the police sergeant. "But what if Cupid came in through the tunnels, like us? He wouldn't be logged with security."

"Judging by the old padlock we had to break to get in, nobody's been in that way for years, so the only alternative is to come through from above. And that would require fairly high level access."

"So it's probably not a student," said Mary.

"Not likely," replied Leopold. "Here we go."

The monitor filled with a long list of time stamps, listing the exact dates and times each time the machine had been accessed.

"Looks like this computer's never been reformatted," said Albert.

"Well, that definitely helps us," said the consultant, peering at the screen. "The last time this machine was used was two days ago, just before midnight."

"That was the day before Christina went missing," said Mary.

"All we have to do now is get to the security files and narrow it down to show who was in the building around the time the email was sent, and who left shortly afterwards. It should be a short list," continued Leopold. "Let's start by giving our security guard friend a quick visit. He's probably wondering where his keys have gotten to by now."

Chapter 26

Leopold's eyes took a moment to readjust to the dim, murky passageway, but his mind was already racing. Now they had a lead. A solid lead. Once they coaxed the entry logs out of the security guard, it would be easy enough to track down Cupid and get some answers. As they reached a tight corner, Jerome called out from behind in a hoarse whisper, and Leopold stopped to turn around.

"I'll go at the front," said Jerome. "Visibility down here is poor, and I should be taking point."

Leopold didn't bother to argue. Directions from Jerome were rarely optional. He stood aside to let the bodyguard pass and took up a following position next to Albert and Mary, who were whispering to each other about something he couldn't quite make out. Albert stopped talking and looked up at him.

"I just wanted to thank you," he said, "for letting me come along with you. It's by far the most fun I've had in years. I honestly thought my tunnelers days were behind me."

"No problem," said Leopold.

"No, really. My life isn't exactly what you'd call… *exciting*. But this, well this is something to tell the grandkids!"

"Don't mention it."

The tour guide beamed and fell quiet as Jerome hissed a warning from ahead. Most of the light bulbs that hung from the tunnel ceiling were either flickering weakly or had gone out altogether.

"Don't move," he whispered. "I heard something up ahead. Follow me. Slowly."

What happened next was almost too fast to register. A sound like a whip crack reverberated through the narrow tunnel as a precise, controlled explosion shattered the stonework off the wall at Jerome's shoulder. The blast threw him sideways, slamming his head against the opposite wall. He slumped to the floor, unconscious. Almost simultaneously, Leopold heard a series of identical blasts erupt behind him, sending shards of stone flying through the passageway in a synchronized series of explosions that snaked down the tunnel walls and across the ceiling like a string of firecrackers. Mary and Albert ducked down, hands clasped over their ears, avoiding the majority of the debris.

A few seconds later, the dust began to clear. The tunnel behind them had collapsed from the force of the explosions, sealing off the way back.

"Is everyone OK?" hissed Leopold.

"What the hell was that?" responded Mary.

"I can't see a thing!" said Albert.

"Jerome's out cold," continued the consultant, his ears ringing, "and the way back is sealed off."

"We have to keep moving," said the police sergeant.

"It's a trap," said Leopold. "Whoever set those explosions wasn't looking to just knock us out; they were meant to kill us and bury us down here."

"So why are we still alive?" asked Albert, shaking slightly.

"Most people would have been killed by that first blast. It was positioned directly at head height. Head height for anyone other than Jerome, anyway. The secondary explosions were to seal off the tunnel. I expect our attacker will collapse the other end once he's inspected his work," said Leopold.

"Inspected his work?" repeated the tour guide nervously.

"He'll be expecting clean kills, but he'll be down to check."

"Then what are we waiting for?" said Mary, "While we have the element of surprise on our side we should go on the offensive."

"Whoa, hold on just a minute," said Albert.

"She's right. There's no other way out. We either wait for him to pick us off in the dark, or we come at him head on. If we're still alive, we can come back for Jerome. Follow me."

Leopold stepped forward and heard Mary pull out her firearm, hoping Albert would be smart enough to stay behind her. The three of them walked forward slowly, toward the basement entrance they had used earlier, trying not to make a sound. The tunnel was nearly completely dark now, most of the lights having been shattered by the blast, and Leopold couldn't see more than a few feet in front of him. The corridor was silent.

The bullet whistled past Leopold's ear and slammed into the wall behind him, throwing up brittle debris as it hit the stone. He dodged to the side instinctively and flattened his back against the wall to avoid a follow up shot. Mary and Albert did the same on the other side of the passageway. Leopold glanced around, feeling the adrenaline kick in, and checked for any sign of movement.

A tiny red dot of light, danced along the opposite wall, seeking out a target. The light made its way closer and closer to where the others were standing, now only partially hidden in the shadows. Leopold knew it was a matter of seconds before they would be forced to break cover and would be in full sight of the gunman. The red dot halted.

Seconds passed and nothing happened. Leopold listened for any sign of movement and caught the sound of fabric rustling about six feet in front of him. Without pausing to think, the consultant shoved against the wall with all his strength and launched himself at the rough area he expected his target to occupy. He lowered his shoulders as he charged to maximize the impact radius of his blow, a technique Jerome had taught him during their training sessions.

Leopold connected. He heard the shooter grunt in surprise and pain as he collided with the man's rib cage, knocking him to the ground. The consultant spun in the darkness, brought the gun to shoulder-level, and adopted a square stance. He lowered the weapon to the ground where the shooter had fallen and aimed. There was nothing there but empty space.

Leopold felt the attack before he saw it. Grasping the consultant's wrist like a vise, the gunman twisted it viciously, pulling his arm behind his back. A sharp blow struck his lower back, throwing him into the wall face first.

Twisting his head to avoid a broken nose, Leopold tasted hot blood as his face connected with the stone. Dropping and rolling, he avoided the attacker's next blow, dodging the impact of the butt of his gun where his head had been just a split second earlier, causing the gunman to grunt with frustration. Glancing up from the floor, the consultant caught one clear glimpse of his attacker as he stood in a stray pool of light.

The man was tall and stocky, and wore a thin trench coat and hat, his features mostly obscured. Leopold recognized him by his strange clothes: one of the passers-by who had caught his attention outside Christina's dorm room. The clothes looked brand new, probably thrown on earlier in the day to provide cover among the other people on the busy streets outside. He could make out several tattoos scrawled in German on the backs of his hands. There were probably matching tattoos under his clothes as well.

Dodging to the side, Leopold avoided Mary as she flew past him and tackled the shooter, knocking the man over and sending his handgun flying across the floor with a clatter. She straddled his chest and brought her own gun around under his chin. The gunman grinned.

"I've not enjoyed being between a woman's legs this much in a long time," he said in a thick German accent, licking his lips slowly.

"Shut up. You have the right to remain silent," Mary began. She never got to finish.

The gunman brought his knee up sharply, connecting with the police sergeant's lower back and throwing her forward. He used her momentum against her and lashed out with his elbow, knocking Mary hard in the ribs and sending her sideways. Rolling off him, she took up a kneeling position and brought her gun around for a second time. Too quickly, the German was off the floor again and he brought a foot down on her shoulder, his heavy boot knocking her violently to the ground, forcing her to release her weapon. He drew a slim, double-edged knife from his belt and grinned again.

"Time to die, bitch."

Rousing all his remaining strength, Leopold lunged, throwing a fist at the man's back as he faced Mary. He connected with soft tissue and felt the man tense as the blow hit home. The German swung his elbow around in retaliation, catching Leopold off balance and knocking him backward against the stone wall. Regaining his composure, the gunman aimed his boot at Mary and connected hard with the side of her head, knocking her out cold. He rounded on Leopold and advanced slowly, knife in hand.

"I think I'll take my time with you," he sneered. "I want you to feel it. Then I want you to watch me kill your girlfriend."

With a cry of frustration, Leopold threw a wild punch, arching the blow in roundhouse fashion to reduce the ability of the gunman to parry. The German brought his elbow up high and took most of the force of the blow to his arm, knocking him off balance but causing no real damage. Desperate, the consultant followed with an uppercut to the stomach, but the gunman dodged and countered by bringing his other elbow around fast, hitting Leopold in the temple. Stars danced across his vision and he once again stumbled against the wall, hands splayed out for balance before toppling to his knees.

His vision cleared, and he saw his attacker throw his crumpled hat to the floor and approach, knife in hand. The blade neared his throat. He could smell sweat and steel. Suddenly, the German let out a cry of surprise as Albert crashed into him, head first, sending them both topping to the ground in a tangled heap.

"Don't you touch my friends!" Albert screamed, throwing his fists feverishly at the man's face.

The German was so surprised he didn't register his attacker at first, but after a few badly aimed punches connected with his jaw, he snapped to his senses and fought back, twisting like a coiled spring. He escaped Albert's grasp with little effort and lashed out in a dazzlingly quick counter-attack of his own.

Albert looked down and saw the blade of the man's knife slide out of his shoulder, releasing a hot, thick flow of blood. His eyes rolled up into his head and he fell backward, unconscious. The attacker laughed, a callous, hoarse laugh, and turned again to face Leopold, brandishing the knife.

"Time to die, Mr. Blake," he said, spitting blood on to the floor.

"Not today," a deep voice echoed from behind.

Stepping into the pool of light, his face mottled with dust and blood, Jerome stood firm and ready. His suit was torn and bloody at the shoulder, but he didn't appear to be in any pain. Sneering, the German lunged, slashing the knife upwards with surgical precision over Jerome's throat, aiming for the jugular.

His smile faltered immediately as the bodyguard caught his wrist and pulled it back sharply, forcing him to drop the weapon. He turned to counter, but Jerome landed a blow to the man's solar plexus with his other hand and sent the gunman toppling to the floor. A well-aimed kick to the man's testicles kept him down for the count, only a writhing groan of pain indicating there was any life left in him.

"I'm fine," said Leopold, as Jerome helped him to his feet. "I'm more concerned about where our friend here is getting his orders."

Nodding, the bodyguard knelt down beside the German, who began breathing normally again. He lifted the knife off the floor and slid the blade between the man's ribs. The gunman screamed in pain.

"The knife is now touching the outside of your lung," Jerome said in a calm voice. "If I apply pressure, the tip of the blade will puncture the parietal pleura, and you really don't want that to happen."

"Go to hell," the bleeding man growled, his face contorted in agony.

"If I press harder still, the knife will completely puncture the lung and you'll pass out from the pain."

He applied a slight pressure to prove his point. The German screamed again.

"Now, let's try this again," said Jerome, leaning closer.

"What – what do you want to know?" the man grunted between quick, shallow breaths.

"Who sent you the order to kill me?" asked Leopold.

"I – I don't know his name. I swear!" he implored as Jerome's expression hardened. "All I know is I get a phone call a few days ago. He tells me he might need my services, and I'll get a call when the time is right. I got the call this morning with your location and followed you here."

"The explosions," said Leopold. "What did you use?"

"I was given something." He pointed at his jacket.

Jerome carefully unzipped the man's leather jacket with his free hand, keeping an even pressure on the knife. He reached into the inside pocket and pulled out a small metal case ten inches in diameter.

"Open it," gasped the gunman.

Jerome snapped open the small case to reveal four small white plastic discs, roughly the same size and shape as a quarter, nestled in black foam like a valuable coin collection. The bodyguard rested the case on the man's chest and pulled one of the discs out, holding it carefully between his thumb and index finger.

"Careful," the man rasped. "You don't want to set those off. Boom."

"What are they?" asked Jerome.

"I don't know their name. They were left for me at the drop point. They have instructions, you just put them down and detonate them with a cell phone. Boom," he laughed hoarsely.

"Are there more? Tell me, who else is coming?" Leopold asked.

The gunman only laughed harder, despite the knife in his side. "You have no idea, do you? I hope they make you suffer, I hope you are awake when they do it. I hope - "

He didn't get to finished his sentence. Jerome pushed the knife deeper into the man's rib-cage, making him howl in pain for several seconds until he passed out, still breathing, but only just. The bodyguard handed the tiny metal case to Leopold.

"Could these really cause all that damage?" Jerome jerked his head back in the direction of the collapsed tunnel.

"Evidently. Though how, exactly, I need to figure out. Nothing a couple hours in the lab can't determine."

"What are we going to do with him?" he looked down at the gunman.

"Leave him here," replied the consultant. "He won't last long without medical attention, and I don't think his employer is going to be too happy about his performance. I doubt we'll be seeing him again."

"What about the others? I don't think I can carry them both, and Albert needs some stitches."

As Leopold considered their next move, he heard Mary and Albert groan quietly as they regained consciousness and he breathed a sigh of relief as they both got to their feet.

"What happened? Is everyone all right?" Mary asked, her voice groggy.

"We're fine," the consultant replied, "though I think Albert might be a little worse for wear."

"Don't worry about me," murmured their tour guide, clutching his shoulder. "It's not bleeding much any more. Just a scratch. Really."

"Good," said Jerome, "I carry a small first aid kit in my jacket that can help with the bleeding. I can get you fixed up, but you'll probably need to go get stitches."

Albert nodded thankfully and squeezed his shoulder a little tighter, turning to Leopold. "What's next?".

"Let's get you fixed up first. Then we'll think about our next move. I've got a feeling we're getting close to finding some answers."

Chapter 27

Leopold helped carry Albert down the tunnel, stopping at one of the bulbs that hadn't been shattered to allow Jerome to inspect the injuries under the hazy light. The bleeding had mostly stopped, leaving a deep, clean gash. The bodyguard dabbed at the wounds gently with a cotton ball and a splash of liquid antibacterial, making his patient flinch in pain. Leopold saw the look of concern on Mary's face.

"Don't worry, he'll be fine."

"I know. It's just that we shouldn't be putting civilians in danger like that."

"Technically, Jerome and I are civilians too."

"That's not the same. You both knew what you were getting into. Albert had no idea. We lied to him and nearly got him killed. Don't you care?"

"Of course I care. I know I don't always exactly speak my mind," he smiled as Mary rolled her eyes in agreement. "I'm not as callous as you think."

"I don't think you're *callous*. I just find you impossible to read, that's all."

"A product of my upbringing, I'm afraid. My father wouldn't approve."

"Letting people know how you feel isn't a weakness. Your father was a good man, but he didn't always get it right when it came to emotions," said Mary, resting her hand on his shoulder, sending a shiver down his spine.

Leopold paused before considering a reply and felt a clawing in his chest. He brushed it off and forced a smile.

"You didn't know him like I did," he said.

Mary squeezed his shoulder, making the hairs on Leopold's forearms stand on end. "It's not your fault, you know," she said softly, looking into his eyes. "No one could have predicted what would happen."

"I should have. The signs were all there."

"Nobody's perfect, Leopold. Not even you. And I still stand by what I said. We'll find out what happened, eventually."

He nodded, and the pair sat in silence as Jerome finished cleaning their tour guide's wound. Albert inspected Jerome's handiwork and gave a thumbs up, then lifted his arm so that a bandage could be fitted.

"What do we do now?" he asked, once Jerome had finished.

"We need to get hold of the security logs that coincide with the time stamps we found on the computer," replied Leopold.

"The security guard's not just going to hand them over," said Albert.

"Let me worry about that," said Mary. "I can be very persuasive."

"Can we avoid any more shooting?"

"No promises," said Jerome.

"We'll try, Albert," said Mary.

Leopold lead the group back through the basement and into the corridors of Uris Hall, each of them squinting as the halogen lights hit their eyes. In less than a minute they had found their way back to the main lobby, the floor littered with scuff marks and dirt from where the fire fighters had trampled through in search of the non-existent emergency. The room was empty, the students having returned to afternoon classes.

"Hey, you! Stop!" a voice rang from the other end of the hall.

Turning, Leopold saw a portly security guard, red-faced and panting, jog over to where they were standing. He reached them after a few seconds of obvious exertion and took a moment to catch his breath.

"You! I know you!" he glared at Mary. "My keys! They went missing after you ran into me outside! What have you done with them?"

"You mean these?" the police sergeant held up a set of keys and jiggled them in front of the guard's face.

"Give them to me!" he reached out a pudgy hand, but Mary drew back out of his grasp.

"Not so fast, Marty," she eyed the guard's security ID badge. "We need a little favor from you."

Marty's face, already red from running across the lobby, turned the color of beetroot. "Give me those keys, now!"

"Not a chance. We need you to do a little search of your security logs and give us the names of everyone who was in this building two days ago at midnight."

Mary dangled the keys again for effect. The fat security guard trembled from what Leopold could only assume was rage. Or perhaps indigestion.

"And just why the hell should I help you? You have exactly two seconds to give those keys back or I'm calling the cops."

She pulled out her badge and held it up to Marty's face. "No need."

He glared at the metal shield and grinned. "I've got your badge number now! Don't think I won't call your boss. You can't just take private property without a warrant. I know the law! You're in big trouble, lady!"

"I don't think so. Let's think about this a minute, Marty. How is this going to look when your boss finds out?" she said, stepping in close.

"Finds out what?"

"That the entire business and economics department was disrupted for the best part of the afternoon. That the fire department had to come out for no good reason, at a cost of several thousand dollars, which I'm sure they'll be billing the University for, and that somebody's been breaking in to Pupin Hall for the past month to send threatening emails from a computer you've got hidden in the basement."

Marty paused a second or two before answering. "What's any of this got to do with me?"

"I'll tell you why you should be worried, Marty. When the board of trustees finds out, they'll want to know who's to blame. I think starting with the security guard who can't keep hold of his keys is a pretty good place to start, don't you?"

The chubby guard blanched, an impressive feat considering his original color. "You wouldn't dare."

"Wouldn't I? A quick call to my contacts in the press and the whole thing goes public in a matter of hours.

How valuable are you to this place that you think you'll be able to keep your job after that?"

Marty opened his mouth to respond, but was quickly cut off as she continued.

"In fact, I'm pretty sure that I'll have some questions for you myself in relation to a recent kidnapping involving someone using University computers to send illegal emails, which would certainly require some help from the inside. So, we can continue this conversation like responsible adults, or I can make a few phone calls."

The rent-a-cop's eyes bulged, but he stayed quiet. After a few seconds he nodded and motioned for them to follow him to his desk. He led the group over to the security office and logged on to the computer. The room was small, with just enough room for Mary and Leopold to lean in over Marty's shoulder and give instructions. Leopold tried not to look at the dog-eared *Playboy* calendars hanging on the wall. Jerome noticed a black windbreaker hanging on the back of the door and held it up to his chest, checking the size.

"Hey, that's mine," said Marty, pointing at Jerome.

The towering bodyguard scowled and pulled off his Armani jacket, revealing his handgun and bloodstained shirt. Marty gulped, and turned his attention back to the computer screen.

"Okay, here you go," coughed Marty, jabbing an oily finger at the monitor. "Two days ago around midnight. Only person to clock out of Pupin is Professor Brian Locke. Works in the Department of Computer Science."

"Where can we find him?" said Leopold.

"He's got a home address listed, but he holds office hours on Friday afternoons, so he won't be there."

"Where's his office?"

"His usual office is at the Shapiro Center, just across campus, but it's being renovated, so they've found him a spare room at Butler Library. You've got about an hour before he locks up for the weekend."

"Good. Mary, I assume this is good enough reason to hold off giving your friends a call about Marty here?"

Mary nodded and handed the keys back to the sweaty guard, who hastily clipped them back onto his belt.

"If this doesn't pan out, I'm coming back for you," she said, pulling aside her jacket to reveal the gun underneath.

Marty glanced at the firearm nervously, then sank back in his chair and sighed deeply. "Don't worry about me. I need this job. If there's anything else you need, just let me know and I'll make it happen."

"I was hoping you'd say that," said Leopold. "I need to borrow one of your labs. There's something I want to take a look at."

Chapter 28

"Fascinating."

The research laboratory was deserted and smelled faintly of sulphur and wood polish. Leopold hunched over a tall microscope, adjusted the focus with his right hand, and waved Jerome over with his left, never taking his eye off the scope. The bodyguard approached, zipping up the windbreaker he had taken from Marty's office. He had tossed the ruined Armani jacket into the laboratory incinerator with some regret.

"Found something?" asked Jerome, peering over Leopold's shoulder.

"Look at this."

The consultant stepped back and Jerome placed his right eye over the lens. "What am I looking at?"

"One of the plastic coins we took from our German friend downstairs," said Leopold. "It's a micro-explosive. I managed to get one open."

"Did you figure out how they work?"

"Oh yes, and they're very clever. Can you see the two reservoirs of liquid?"

"Yes; what are they?"

"This is the clever bit. It uses a binary explosive to create a potent detonation that is restricted to a very small radius – perfect for targeted attacks with little or no collateral damage. You take two chemicals, either of which is harmless by itself, and mix them together to form a volatile explosive. Add a battery and circuit board, and you can detonate remotely. I can't tell which chemicals have been used here without further testing, but I'm guessing nitromethane and ethylenediamene."

"How does it work?"

"When the device receives the signal, it releases an electric charge strong enough to melt the layer of resistor-impregnated plastic that separates the two chemicals. After a few seconds, the chemicals mix and a second signal is sent, which triggers another charge and detonates the device."

"I've never heard of something like this," said Jerome, still squinting into the microscope.

"It's cutting-edge stuff. This sort of technology isn't around in the public domain yet. These must be the prototypes that were stolen from the military facility a few days ago."

The bodyguard stood up straight again, his face grim. "There's enough of the chemicals stored in this capsule to blow a hole in solid rock. Just think what that would do if you planted it on a person."

Albert started patting his pockets frantically, his eyes bulging in horror as his fingers found what turned out to be his keys. "Phew! Sorry guys, carry on."

"That's certainly a possibility," replied Leopold. "Considering how small they are, it would be almost impossible to notice someone slipping them into a bag or coat. They don't give off any radiation, and they use the same radio technology as cell phones, so they'd be difficult to detect by scanning devices. In short, the perfect anti-personnel explosive for busy urban areas."

"How many are left?" asked Jerome.

"There were three recovered from our friend in the tunnels, so we've got two left that I haven't dissected. I'll be holding on to those for further study; they don't have all the equipment here that I need to determine the exact composition of the chemicals."

"Make sure you keep them in their case. I don't want to have to scoop you off the sidewalk."

"Don't worry, they're harmless without the remote trigger. I could smash them with a hammer and still not set them off."

Leopold closed the lid of the metal case holding the remaining two micro-bombs and slipped it into his jacket pocket. He buttoned his jacket and motioned for the others to follow him.

"It's time we found Professor Locke," he said, turning off the light to the microscope. "Office hours are officially open."

Chapter 29

It was four P.M. and the sun was still bright in the sky above the Columbia University lawns, though the air had cooled and the wind had blown away the smell of hot asphalt from earlier in the day. Leopold led the others toward Butler Library with a quick, determined step and ran over the events of the day in his head.

"Penny for your thoughts?" Mary sidled up beside him.

Snapping out of his daze, he looked around as they continued walking. She was wearing that warm smile that had always been so effective at disarming him in the past.

"Just running through the facts of the case in my head," he replied.

"Any conclusions?"

"None at this point. On the one hand, there's at least one person who wants me dead. On the other, we have only a few hours to track down a kidnapped girl before she ends up dead, and our only lead is just a few hundred feet away."

"Not our only lead," said Mary. "You already said you didn't trust the senator, so maybe he's involved somehow."

"Possibly. I know he's hiding something, but I'm not sure what. But I am sure he's no killer. He could have taken me out at his house this morning if he'd wanted me dead."

"Then who else would try taking you out?"

"The list is almost endless. Being in my line of work doesn't exactly make you new friends," said Leopold, smiling grimly.

Mary nodded and rubbed her arms as the wind picked up, her thin jacket providing little protection. Leopold wondered where the warmth of the morning had gone and gritted his teeth a little.

"So what's the plan?" said Albert, trotting up to join them, leaving Jerome to take up the rear.

"According to Marty, Professor Locke's office is on the sixth floor, behind the rare books and manuscripts collection," said Leopold. "I'll need to make sure no students barge in on us, so I'll need someone to watch the corridors near the office and stop anyone trying to get in."

"I'll do it," said Albert, enthusiastically.

"Are you sure you're up to it? You're still injured," said Leopold.

Albert nodded animatedly. "It's fine. The bleeding's stopped and the pain killers Jerome gave me are doing a great job. Let me do this. I can help!"

Mary caught Leopold's eye. He knew it was a risk to put Albert in danger again, especially after he had been nearly killed in the tunnels, but he didn't foresee any real issues. He put a hand on Albert's uninjured shoulder as they walked.

"Okay. But I don't want you playing the hero again, understand? At the first sign of trouble, come and get us. You're not trained to handle situations like before, and it could get you killed."

"I'm fine! And besides, I reckon I saved your life. Without me, who knows what that sicko would have done."

Pausing for a moment, the consultant turned to face Albert. "You're right, I owe you a debt of gratitude. If you ever need anything from me, just ask. I officially owe you one."

The group reached the heavy wooden doors that opened out into the entrance lobby of the library. The doorway itself was nearly twenty feet high, but was dwarfed by the fourteen enormous columns above that helped support the library's hulking stone frame and its contents of nearly two million books.

Inside, the cavernous main hall rose over three stories from the polished floor to the gilded ceiling, with long, three-tiered chandeliers that hung at regular intervals across the room. Despite the ornate lighting, the room received most of its illumination from the tall windows that stretched the height of the walls, letting in enough sun that Leopold wondered why the lights were switched on at all. The library smelled of cold stone and polished oak, and was silent enough that he felt a little self-conscious breathing. The only faint noises were the soft clacks of computer keyboards and the scribble of pens and pencils on notepads.

After a short ride in the elevators, the doors opened out onto the sixth floor of the library and Leopold set off in the direction of the faculty offices, with the others close behind.

The rare books and manuscripts section was more modern than many of the other areas of the library, with controlled lighting and glass-fronted display cabinets stretching out the full length of the corridors. As they walked through, Leopold glanced with interest at the selection of ancient texts, artwork, and tablets that sat behind the reinforced displays.

"There's over four thousand years of history housed up here," he said. "And around fourteen miles of manuscripts stored alongside about half a million books detailing the entirety of human civilization. Right here is the culmination of all mankind's achievements since we learned how to write."

"Thanks for the history lesson," said Mary. "I'll be sure to check something out on the way back. Do you think they'll give me a library card?"

He gave up and sighed. "Just don't touch anything."

"Roger that." She gave a mock-salute and rolled her eyes.

They soon found the office area, exactly as Marty had described. There were five offices in total, each facing out onto a central reading area with three tables and some scattered chairs. The only sound was the buzz of an overhead neon light in its final throes and the soft thrum of the air conditioning. Leopold spotted Locke's office in the far corner, just a windowless door with his name written in magic marker on a scrap of paper and taped to the wood. Leopold knocked gently.

"Come in," a muffled voice came from inside.

Leopold opened the door and stepped inside, followed closely by the others. Professor Locke's office was a mess, with boxes of stacked papers lining the edges of the walls and loose manuscripts and battered textbooks scattered around the floor. Locke himself stood with his shirt sleeves rolled up, sweating from what Leopold assumed was the effort of unpacking all the heavy books. The professor was short and overweight. His dark hair was slicked back with greasy hair gel, and his white shirt was littered with various stains, both old and new, all of varying color. Set on one of the shelves where he had finished unpacking was a half-eaten sandwich. The room smelled like mustard.

"What do you want?" Locke asked, leaning against the bookshelf and wiping his brow with the back of his forearm.

"Professor Brian Locke?" asked Leopold

"Yeah. Like I said, what do you want? You ain't students of mine, and I got work to do."

"We're here to talk to you about Christina Logan. One of your students, right?" said Leopold, taking a step forward.

"Who wants to know?"

"My name is Leopold Blake, and this is Mary Jordan of the NYPD. The tall gentleman is my security officer, Jerome, and this is a private consultant, Albert Fitzgerald. We're working with Christina's father, Senator Logan."

Locke took a deep breath and slowly exhaled, contemplating. He picked up the unfinished sandwich and took a large bite, dropping crumbs onto his already-filthy shirt. He continued speaking with his mouth full.

"Yeah, that'sh me. What'sh thish all about?"

"When was the last time you saw Christina?" asked Leopold.

Locke finished his mouthful of sandwich and made a smacking noise. He kept the rest in his hand as he spoke, pausing only to wipe his mouth.

"Erm… Must have been a couple days ago during class. Why? Where is she?"

"She's been kidnapped," said Mary, holding up her police shield.

Locke dropped his sandwich. "Wh – what? Is she okay?"

"We have evidence that you were sending Christina threatening emails. Can you explain?"

"No! I w – wouldn't! She's a student of mine. Why would I want to do that?"

"The computer in the basement. I have a copy of the entire hard drive, along with security records of you in the building at the time the emails were sent."

Locke began to sweat, tiny beads of perspiration forming on his greasy brow. Jerome cracked his knuckles and Locke flinched slightly, considering his options.

"Okay, okay! I admit it! I sent her some… unsavory emails. But I would never hurt her!" said the professor, palms up.

"What relationship existed between you and Christina?"

"There was no relationship. Nothing more than professor and student."

"Then why send those messages? Were you in love with her?"

"I – I asked her out once. She said no."

"That's it?" said Mary, folding her arms.

"W – well, I asked her out again and she got pretty mad. Threatened to report me to the dean. Little bitch. I got a little mad," said Locke, avoiding the police sergeant's stare.

"The last email said that you knew some kind of secret. What did that mean?"

"N – nothing! I was just... bluffing! Wanted to scare her a little, that's all. I swear!"

Mary frowned. "You're lying, Brian. Tell us the truth."

"I'm not lying!" he said, trembling.

"Your voice raises in pitch by several tones when you lie," said Leopold, interrupting. "You also stutter, and you can't stop playing with your hands."

Locke looked down at his hands and shoved them into his pockets. "Fine. Ask your damn questions."

"There's only one thing I'm interested in," said Leopold. "Tell me about this so-called family secret. Then I'll decide what to do with you."

Locke slumped in his desk chair and took a deep breath. "There was a fundraising benefit held at the University last month, and my department was invited. I noticed that Christina and her father were there as well, so naturally I kept and eye on them during the meal." He paused.

"Keep going," said Leopold.

"I first noticed something was a little odd when I went to the bathroom just after the appetizers. I remember, it was this really great French onion soup with the nicest little –"

"Get to the point, Brian," said Mary.

"Oh – right. Yeah, so I go to the bathroom and I see these guys out in the hallway, all dressed up in business suits and looking like they were waiting for someone. I heard one of them mention Logan's name. Sounded like they were pretty desperate to speak to him."

"So, what happened?"

"Well, I went back to the table and waited for the senator to get up and leave. Then I followed him. He met with the guys in the suits and they went into a room together. It all felt a little cloak and dagger to me, so I listened in."

"Go on."

"I went into the room next door and put my ear against the wall, which was pretty thin. I heard the senator getting really agitated about something to do with raising money, and I heard one of the others tell him that they couldn't help him without a show of good faith, or something like that. They pretty much stopped talking after that, so I slipped back to my table before anyone noticed I'd been gone too long."

"Then what?" said Leopold.

"Nothing more happened at the dinner, but when I got home I looked up some of the details of the organization running the fundraiser. Turns out the company is a subsidiary of a corporation owned by a private equity firm that invests on the behalf of a trust fund. And you can guess who the beneficiary to the fund is."

"Senator Logan," said Leopold.

"Damn right! Seems a bit of a coincidence that a charity event set up to help starving children or whatever was managed by a company that one of the major donors actually owns. Smells pretty rotten to me. So I did some digging and found about a dozen other cases where a company owned or part-owned by the senator was involved in some kind of baloney charity deal," said Locke.

"What do you mean, 'baloney'?" asked Mary.

"Keep up, honey. For every fundraiser his company organizes, the senator makes a large cash donation in his own name. The charity's sponsors match the donation into one of the company's holding accounts," said Locke. "Next, the company pipes the money through enough fake accounts to make sure nobody can trace it, and then skims a huge amount off the top. The charity ends up receiving about 25% of the total money raised. The whole thing is a massive front."

"How did you find all this out?"

"I'm a professor in Columbia University's computer science department, one of the leading centers for research in the world. I know a few people who can do useful things with computers," said Locke, sarcastically.

"Okay, so why was the senator so agitated at the dinner, if he's getting so much money?"

"Who knows? Could be that whatever he's into requires a hell of a lot more than he can raise. That's my theory."

"So why email Christina?" asked Mary.

"I figured I could email Christina and really freak her out. After she realizes what dear old dad has done, she tells her father about the emails and then I propose a meeting. That way I can put Daddy's little angel in her place, *and* expose the senator for the fraud that he is."

"Unless the senator happens to change your mind somehow," said Leopold, raising his eyebrows.

"You mean blackmail?" replied Locke, in mock horror. "I prefer the term *financial persuasion*. Besides, how is it different from accepting campaign donations from companies wanting to affect government policy? I say it's about time politicians started listening to taxpayers like me!"

"We're not here to discuss politics. Why did you go to so much trouble to hide your tracks?" said Leopold.

"Are you kidding? The whole point was to harass Christina enough so that I'd eventually get through to her father, who's not exactly going to be overjoyed at the whole thing. Senator Logan could find a guy like me in a matter of minutes if he wanted to. So, unless I hide what I'm doing, I'm dead meat."

"You might still be," said Mary.

"Huh? What do you mean?" said the professor.

"Christina was kidnapped by the same person who murdered three senators in cold blood. Chances are he already knows who you are, and he'll be wanting to know what you know. There's someone out there, someone dangerous, who isn't going to want any loose ends. Catch my drift?"

All the color drained out of Locke's face, and his jaw fell open. He didn't make a noise for a moment and then suddenly began to hyperventilate.

"Calm down, Professor Locke," said Mary, rolling her eyes. "If you cooperate with us, I can offer you police protection."

"W – what do you want me to do?" asked the flustered professor, panting.

"We have a special job in mind for you," said Leopold. "But first, I need some time to think. You need to stay here in case any of your students show up for office hours and people start wondering where you are. In the mean time, where's the nearest room we can use?"

"Erm… j – just round the corner. G – go left out of here and through the double doors. It sh – should be empty," said Locke, trying to control his breathing.

"Good. We'll be back soon. Don't move."

Chapter 30

Leopold found the empty classroom, a narrow and windowless space, and shut the door behind him. The others each took a seat at the table as Leopold picked up a pen and scribbled bullet points on the whiteboard. Jerome shuffled uncomfortably in the small chair, which creaked under the strain.

"What are we doing in here?" asked Mary. "We should be following up on Professor Locke's statement."

"We have no reason to assume he's not telling the truth," said Leopold. "His statement hardly paints him as the virtuous type. He could go to prison just for sending the emails, let alone hacking into private bank accounts and blackmailing a state senator. If that story was devised to clear his name, I'd say he failed miserably."

"Point taken. What are you writing?"

"I have a theory."

"Okay, shoot."

Leopold finished writing on the whiteboard and stood to the side, pointing at each line as he spoke. "First, we take the kidnapping case in isolation and ignore the murders. The majority of kidnappings are committed for financial gain, with some carried out to further a political agenda, for revenge, or sometimes just for sick thrills. As the kidnapper demanded a ransom, we can rule out the second reason."

The others all nodded in agreement, and he moved on to the second point. "However, when the exchange was supposed to happen, the kidnapper and Christina disappeared. Why leave all that money behind? The only explanation is that the motive for the kidnapping was no longer financial."

"Why would a kidnapper change his motive halfway through?" asked Mary.

"He wouldn't. Someone who has gone to this much trouble is hardly going to alter his tactics at the most crucial moment unless the kidnapper himself were no longer in the picture. What if there were actually two kidnappers, acting independently? Each of them with their own agenda. The second kidnapper could have somehow managed to get Christina away from the first. There's going to be at least one dead body in this scenario."

"Hank," said Mary.

"Exactly. Kidnapper number one. Problem is, it's very difficult to question a corpse. Fortunately, the bank details we found at his house should be enough to eventually trace where that money came from."

"Hang on, this doesn't make any sense. Why would someone pay a kidnapper in advance?"

"You get an 'A', Ms. Jordan! It makes no sense to pay ransom to a kidnapper in advance. However, something Locke said put the last piece of the puzzle into place."

"And that was?"

"Consider the facts. Senator Logan is desperate to find Christina's kidnapper, and he only brings us in once he loses control of the situation, which I found a little irregular. Add to that his secretive demeanor during our first meeting, and my suspicions were aroused immediately. Locke's story regarding the senator's desperate need for a large amount of cash only confirmed my suspicions were correct."

"Okay, so how does it all fit together?" asked Mary.

"Remember the senator talked about the insurance policy he had in place to cover kidnappings? It would be relatively straightforward for him to pay somebody to stage a kidnapping of his daughter, hand over the cash, and then receive the settlement from the insurance company. He then gets the cash back from his accomplice and he's effectively doubling his money."

"But Christina's father didn't even know about Hank. How could he have set it up?"

"According to Christina's friends, the relationship between her and Hank was secret," said Leopold. "However, I doubt a man of Senator Logan's status and wealth leaves anything involving his daughter to chance. I'd be very surprised if he didn't have security keeping tabs on Christina twenty-four hours a day. Judging by Hank's character, it probably wouldn't have been too difficult to convince him to stage the kidnapping in return for a modest sum. In this case, twenty thousand dollars from a shell corporation that's likely part of the senator's charity scam."

"Couldn't Hank just keep the cash once the exchange went down?" asked Mary.

"Technically, yes. But I doubt he'd be alive for very long afterwards to enjoy it. Logan no doubt put some security measures in place to make sure he got the cash back," said Leopold.

"But why go to all this trouble?" asked Albert. "It sounds like the senator is rich enough as it is."

"The only thing Logan craves more than money is power. With enough support, Logan has a shot at the U.S. Senate, and from there maybe even the White House. We already know he has friends in all the right places. The only thing he needs is financial assistance, given that your average run for office can rack up bills in the hundreds of millions."

"All this just to further a career?" said Mary.

"People have died for far less."

"This all sounds a little farfetched. We can't just accuse Senator Logan without rock-solid evidence," said Mary, folding her arms.

"Evidence will come now that we know where to look. Subpoena the accounts in question, starting with the fake charities, and you'll find the paper trail. There'll be phone records too, linking Hank to all of this. I doubt he had the brains to cover his tracks properly," said Leopold. "Find the one puzzle piece that fits, and the rest will all fall into place."

"But that still doesn't help us figure out where Christina is now. If you're saying a second kidnapper has her, how do we find them? We don't even know who this person is."

"On the contrary, I know exactly who has Christina. It's the same person who's been sending people after us all day, trying to put us out of service."

"And who's that?"

Leopold wrote the name in large letters on the whiteboard.

Chapter 31

Stark knocked on the door to the senator's bedroom and stepped inside without waiting for a response. They were at least an hour behind schedule, and the colonel was eager to put the next phase of the plan into effect. Logan still sat at his desk, the glow of the computer monitors bathing the dark room in a murky glow. Stark took a few steps toward the senator, who was cradling his head in his hands and breathing deeply.

"Sir? It's time to move. We're late for your appointment in the city," said Stark.

The senator didn't reply.

"Sir? We have to move. Now."

Logan lifted his head slowly, and turned around in the chair to face his head of security. The senator's face was drawn and his eyes were bloodshot, strained from glaring into a computer monitor for most of the day.

"What's the point, Stark?" Logan mumbled. "It's all for nothing. If I show up this afternoon without the money, it's all over."

The colonel suppressed a sigh. *This wasn't how it was supposed to go.* He wondered whether another approach would yield better results.

"There's more, sir," said Stark, flatly. "We tracked Blake to the source of the threatening emails. It seems one of the University's professors had been planning to blackmail you. He discovered your involvement with some charitable donations that went missing and had wanted to use this as leverage."

The senator's eyes widened. He opened his mouth to speak, but no words came out.

"And it's only a matter of time before Blake gathers enough evidence to link you to your daughter's kidnapping," continued the soldier. "He already found the cash you transferred to Hank. It'll be easy enough for him to trace the money back to you."

Senator Logan began to tremble. "You – you know about all those things?"

"Of course," said Stark. "Within twelve hours of installing my team here, I knew everything about you. Your misguided political ambitions are overshadowed only by your greed and corruption. How could a man put his own daughter in danger, just to further his career?"

"Sh – she was never in danger. H – Hank is harmless."

"Hank *was* harmless," said Stark. "Viktor took care of him the night Christina disappeared. Unfortunately, Hank was stupid enough to call in the ransom demand while your daughter was slutting it up in a nightclub in front of a dozen witnesses. Thanks to Hank, three other people had to die so that I could have Christina to myself."

"Wh – what are you talking about?" said the senator, his eyes suddenly sharp.

"I can't believe our nation's leaders can really be this stupid," said the colonel, his lip twisting into a sneer. "I had originally planned on just getting a little intel from you before I killed you, but once I uncovered your little plan I decided to wait. It's people like you that have corrupted this country, and I plan on cleaning up. Starting with you and your business partners, who you were so kind to introduce me to."

"My daughter! Wh – why do you want to hurt her?" said Logan, his voice trembling in horror.

"Her name is Christina," said Stark, raising his voice. "And you put her in danger the minute you decided her life was worth less than your own blind ambition. She's a necessary casualty in this war. But her sacrifice will not be forgotten."

Logan jumped from his seat and dashed for the open door. Stark grabbed him by the collar, throwing him back into the chair. The senator landed hard and let out a yelp.

"If only you had stuck to the plan and come with me into the city an hour ago," said the colonel, almost regretfully, "I might have let you live a little longer. As it is, I can get by without you. Your business associates will just have to wait for now."

Stark pulled his gun from its holster and pressed it against the senator's forehead. "I don't normally go in for showmanship, but I think I'll make an exception. This is a large-caliber Glock 37 with a .45 caliber bore. Its hollow point will expand on impact for maximum damage. The reason I'm telling you this is that I want you to know what's going to happen to you now."

The senator's whole body was shaking, and Stark noticed a puddle forming on the carpet underneath the chair. The great senator Logan had pissed himself. The colonel grabbed the desk chair and spun the senator around, lifting the gun from the senator's forehead and pressing it against the back of his skull instead.

"When I squeeze the trigger," Stark continued, "the bullet will smash through your skull and into your brain before you've even heard the gunshot. The soft tip will expand on impact, tearing through the insides of your head and opening an exit wound the size of a softball, splashing your brains all over your bedroom wall."

Logan began to whimper quietly.

Stark continued. "The best part is that your face will be gone, so you'll need a closed casket at the funeral, and you'll die knowing that your family won't be able to look you in the eyes. Or what's left of them."

The senator began to weep uncontrollably, his body heaving up and down. "P – please d – don't do this."

Stark had learned long ago to blank out the desperate pleas of the men he killed. Many had begged for their lives and the lives of their families. Most had not deserved to die, but Stark had been able to summon the courage to do his duty. Now, standing with a gun pressed to the head of a corrupt politician, Stark recognized the evil he had once thought existed only in the darkest recesses of war. This was not a man fighting to protect his country. This was not a man forced to kill to preserve his family's way of life. This was a man who wanted to take that life away.

Stark pulled the trigger without another thought.

Chapter 32

"Stark? The senator's security chief?" said Mary. "What makes you think he has anything to do with this?"

"He's the only one that fits," said Leopold, pointing to the whiteboard. "The murders were all committed by a professional, and Stark certainly has the pedigree."

"What about motive?"

"A disgraced former black ops colonel would hold a grudge against anyone remotely connected to current military policy. He truly believes he's doing the country a favor by getting rid of what he considers to be corrupt leadership," said Leopold. "But motive is irrelevant. He's the only person with the skill and opportunity to pull this off."

"Why not just kill Senator Logan? He's had plenty of opportunity," said Mary. "I don't see the benefit in going after Christina."

"This is an opportunity to twist the knife and really make Logan suffer. On top of that, he also gets a hostage he can use if things go wrong."

Albert stood up suddenly, his index finger raised in the air as though to emphasize his point. "Just one question."

"Yes?" said Leopold.

"Stark is the one who has Christina and has been sending people to try and kill us?"

"That's right."

"So he's also the same person who's been following us all day, knows our exact location, and has a team of expertly trained soldiers at his command?"

Leopold paused a moment before saying anything. "I see your point," he said eventually.

"So, what the hell do we do now there's a small army on our tail?" said Albert.

"May I make a suggestion?" said Jerome quietly.

"Please do," said the tour guide, trying to remain calm.

"Tactically, we still have one advantage. Stark isn't aware of how much we know, which gives us time to formulate an offensive strategy that will catch him off guard," said Jerome.

"Sounds risky. What if they get away with Christina, or she gets hurt in the process?" said Mary.

"Stark won't risk hurting Christina – she's his only bargaining chip. Our priority has to be getting the police and FBI on our side," said the bodyguard.

"What's the first move?" said Mary.

"We need to get back to Hank's apartment and collect any evidence we can find before Stark gets a chance to destroy it. That should give us leverage with the FBI if he decides to make a run for it. We'll need their resources to track him," said the bodyguard.

Leopold and Mary both nodded in agreement, while Albert fiddled nervously with his shirt sleeves. Leopold wiped the board clean and drew a crude map of NYC, marking their current location at the University in red and Hank's apartment in blue.

"Hank's apartment is just a couple of miles away, maybe ten minutes in the car if we don't hit traffic," said the consultant, tapping the board. "We know that Stark has spotters throughout the city who've been tracking our movements, so we'll only have a few minutes to get what we need from inside."

"What about the nutty professor in there?" Mary jabbed her thumb at the door.

"Bring him. He's the only one who knows all the details about the senator's scams with the fake charities, so as far as I'm concerned, he's our star witness. Let's get moving."

Leopold pushed back his chair and rose to his feet, leading the group back to Professor Locke's office. The door was ajar, and the consultant pushed through without knocking. He stopped dead as he saw what was waiting for him.

Professor Locke was slumped face-down over his desk, with the hilt of a large knife protruding from the back of his neck. Blood pooled around his head and dripped slowly onto the carpet. Mary stepped forward to examine the body as Leopold stood in the doorway. She reached down and felt for a pulse.

"So much for our star witness," she said.

Somewhere behind him, Leopold heard a soft metallic *click* and wheeled around to see the barrel of submachine gun staring him in the face.

CHAPTER 33

Leopold felt Jerome yank him backward just a split second before he saw the gun's barrel flash and heard the deafening *bang* of the first rounds just inches from his face. From what Leopold could tell, the rounds whistled harmlessly over his head and smacked into the wall at the far end of the room.

As Leopold felt himself fall to the ground, he saw the bodyguard kick out with his right leg, slamming the door in the shooter's face.

"Get down!" yelled Jerome, and the others hit the carpet.

Just as Mary drew her weapon and covered the top of her head with her free hand, the sound of splintering wood his Leopold's ears as more bullets ripped through the door, shattering it from its hinges. Jerome gestured silently and the others all rolled to the left, out of the way. The bodyguard crouched just to the side of the door frame and waited.

Nothing.

What remained of the battered door flew from the frame as a heavy black boot smashed through. In the doorway stood a man dressed in dark body armor, complete with helmet and visor, holding a submachine gun with both hands. As the armed soldier stepped into the room he saw a reflection in the glass of one of the cabinets and wheeled around. As he did so, Jerome rose quickly and aimed his elbow at the soft, exposed area between the man's collar and helmet. Leopold heard a damp crunch followed by a muffled whimper as the bodyguard followed up with a heavy punch to the ribs, knocking his opponent to the ground. Jerome grabbed either side of the helmet and yanked the man's head backward and to the side, breaking his neck. He checked for a pulse and got back to his feet, eyes sharp and alert.

"Who the hell was that?" asked Mary.

"One of Stark's men," said Leopold, breathing heavily. "Sent in to tie up any loose ends. Stark must have tracked us here."

"That means he knows we're coming for him."

"We're screwed!" said Albert. "How are we supposed to get the evidence we need now?"

"We still need to go to Hank's apartment," said Leopold. "It's our only option. This just means getting there's going to be a little more difficult, that's all."

"Are you freakin' kidding me?" said the tour guide. "There's no chance we're getting there alive."

"I don't see how we have a choice," said Mary, "We need that evidence. The alternative is to wait here until we get picked off one by one. Are you coming, or would you rather stay here by yourself?"

Albert gulped and nodded feverishly as Jerome headed for the door. "I'm coming! Wait up!"

Jerome took the lead with the others close behind. The group proceeded slowly, while the bodyguard checked ahead for danger, and soon passed through the doors into the rare manuscript section. Jerome motioned for everyone to crouch.

"We're not far from the elevators," hissed Albert, pointing ahead. "Looks like the path is clear."

"Negative," replied the bodyguard, his voice barely audible. "They'll have the elevators covered. We need to get to the stairwell, which should be narrow enough to funnel everyone into single-file. No advantage in numbers that way."

"But –"

Jerome put his finger to his lips, and gestured in the direction of the reading room, just past the glass doors ahead of them. The room stretched the entire width of the library and was stacked to the ceiling with leather-bound books, scrolls, and manuscripts all arranged neatly on shelves behind glass cabinets. The floor space was mostly filled with desks and chairs, and in the middle of the room stood an antique printing press, protected by a silk rope.

Leopold noticed movement just behind the printing press and kept his head down. There were at least three of Stark's team standing just a few feet away, and the only way to the stairwell was right under their noses. Both Jerome and Mary drew their firearms silently, checking the chambers for ammunition.

"There's maybe a fifty percent chance these guys know we're on the move," whispered the bodyguard. "But if we wait much longer and their buddy doesn't check in, we're one hundred percent fucked."

Leopold always hated it when Jerome swore. It usually meant they were thirty seconds away from a near-death experience.

"Mary, I need you to flank to the right," hissed Jerome. "I'll take the left. Leopold, Albert, I need you both to crouch behind that desk in the middle and wait for my signal. The element of surprise is all we've got right now."

Mary signaled her agreement, and the bodyguard slid forward silently and pushed open the glass doors into the reading room. He disappeared off to the left and Mary to the right, using the desks as cover. Leopold took Albert by the arm, slipped through the doors behind them, and crouched on the floor as directed, under cover and out of sight.

"Wait here," said Leopold. "I'm not in the mood for hiding today."

Albert nodded and didn't try to argue. Leopold left him sitting under the desk and headed after Mary, keeping low and trying not to make any noise. As he passed a large cabinet he caught sight of the police sergeant ahead of him, also low to the ground with her weapon drawn. Pushing back the tingle of fear, he pressed ahead and caught up as she stopped to check her target's position. As he approached, she whipped around and raised her gun, eyes wide and jaw set.

"What the hell are you doing?" Mary whispered, lowering the gun.

"Albert doesn't need a babysitter, and I've already nearly got you killed once already today. I can help."

"That's bullshit. Albert definitely *does* need a babysitter."

"Well, I'm here now."

"Fine. Just keep quiet and stay behind me."

Leopold nodded and focused his gaze ahead as he noticed a shadow crossing the floor about ten feet from where they were hiding. He pointed it out to Mary, who nodded and raised her gun in both hands. The two of them moved forward in a crouched position until they reached the end of the row of desks.

Leopold strained over Mary's shoulder for a view of their target, who was facing away from them with both hands resting on his submachine gun. Like the other, he was wearing dark body armor and a helmet, meaning his hearing would be impaired. Leopold glanced at Mary, who seemed to be thinking the same thing.

The seconds crawled by, dragged out interminably by the clawing silence of the library. Leopold could hear his own heartbeat thumping. He could hear Mary's breath beside him, coming in shallow whispers. The man in the armor turned and paced back toward them slowly, stopping just short of their hiding place. He turned around again. Surveying the room.

Rising quickly and silently, Mary brought her gun around and pressed it hard against the armored man's exposed neck, just underneath his ear. At the same time she brought her free arm around the front of his chest, pinning his arms. Leopold saw the man stiffen as he realized what was happening, and then Mary brought her foot down on the inside of the man's knee joint, forcing him to the floor. She coaxed the weapon away from him and hissed for him to lie face down with his hands above his head. He complied. She pulled off his helmet and brought the butt of her gun down on the back of his head and the man fell unconscious. She removed his radio and fished a plastic cable tie from her pocket and zipped it around the man's wrists, behind his back.

A scuffling sound came from the other end of the room, and Leopold turned to see Jerome walk toward them, unharmed.

"Area secured," said Jerome, brushing himself down.

"Let's keep moving," said Mary. "There are probably others on the way."

The group turned to make their way back to the corridor that led to the stair wells. As they passed by the printing press near the center of the room, Leopold heard the crackle of a two-way radio. A voice spluttered on the other end and three other voices replied, checking in with the team leader.

"Four more," said Leopold.

"In the building," replied Jerome. "There may be more outside waiting."

Leopold heard a rustle from the far end of the room, near the exit, and froze. He sensed the others do the same. The noise grew louder, followed by the sound of something hard hitting a wooden surface.

"Ow!"

Albert stood up at the far end of the room, his head and shoulders just about visible above the desk partitions, and rubbed his forehead.

"Hey, guys, I'm sorry I missed all the action!" he called out.

Leopold hissed at him to keep quiet, but before Albert could register what was going on, four dark figures burst through the doors behind him. Leopold leapt to the side as the bullets began to fly. He saw Mary and Jerome do the same. He landed hard and felt a sharp pain in his side, probably a cracked rib, but he summoned enough strength to push back the pain and made his way to the edge of the room, sheltering behind the desks. He saw Mary and Jerome do the same, on the opposite side, mostly hidden by bookshelves. The antique printing press obscured the rest of his view.

He kept low and heard the shuffle of footsteps hurrying in his direction, making out two distinct pairs heading his way. As the footsteps neared, he peered out from around the corner of the desk to get a view of his attackers.

Two men stood in single file in the tight gap between the desks and the wall. They were dressed in the same armor as the others, both carrying the same weapons. He noticed them glance to the side, momentarily distracted by the sound of a muffled grunt from the other side of the room.

Leopold seized the opportunity and attacked, aiming low and slamming his palm into the side of the man's knee joint where there was no armor. Leopold felt the cartilage crunch as the impact forced the patella out of place. His target dropped like a stone, too surprised to make a noise. Without wasting a second, Leopold stood and unclipped the man's helmet, swinging it hard at the second attacker's shoulder.

The helmet was heavy enough to knock the second assailant off balance, and Leopold used the momentum to swing the helmet back around, slamming it hard into the back of the first man's skull where the bone was weakest. He felt the impact through his arm and heard a wet smack as the base of the disabled soldier's skull caved in and he fell forward, gurgling. Leopold brought the helmet around once again and aimed for the second man's head. He connected, and forced the helmet down over the man's eyes, blinding him. In retaliation, the armored soldier kicked out with a heavy boot and caught Leopold in the gut, doubling him over and sending him crashing into a nearby desk. The boot's owner grunted in frustration, before he finally wrenched off his helmet and threw it to the floor, exposing a scarred face and a shock of white-blond hair. Leopold recognized his attacker from his visit to the senator's home several hours earlier: *Dolph*.

Leopold fought back the pain in his chest where the boot had landed and forced himself forward, shoulders low. He connected before his opponent could fire, knocking him off balance. He kept pushing until they hit one of the bookcases, slamming Dolph's back against the shelves and shattering the glass. The submachine gun fell to the ground, and Leopold kicked it away. No good for close range.

Dolph punched Leopold's chest and stomach with quick, short jabs designed for maximum impact. Leopold bunched his arms, shielding himself as though he were boxing. The jabs came fast and hard, and Leopold twisted so that some of the force was absorbed by the softer tissue in his upper arm instead of his neck or face. Still hurt like hell. Dolph pushed back, using his larger frame to drive Leopold toward the center of the room. A final hard shove and Leopold went over one of the desks. He landed with a thump on the other side, which sent a searing flash of pain across his body as the impact jarred his damaged ribs.

The enormous blond rounded the desk and made straight for Leopold. He hadn't bothered picking up the gun. Before he could get up, Dolph aimed a kick to Leopold's stomach, sending him sliding across the hard floor with a gasp of pain. A second kick knocked him against the wooden frame of the antique printing press. He balled up and the third kick landed to his shoulder, turning him onto his back.

Dolph's next kick was aimed at the head, but Leopold twisted away at the last second and his attacker's boot connected the printing press with a loud *thud*. The force of the kick must have shattered at least one toe, but the scarred giant didn't make a sound to indicate he'd felt it. Leopold kicked out at Dolph's shin and knocked him off balance, giving him the chance to get to his feet, where he took a split second to catch his breath.

The two of them faced each other, and Dolph advanced with his fists raised, jabbing at Leopold's face, until the two men were toe to toe. Leopold weaved nimbly between the blows, taking advantage of his opponent's slower movements, and shot both hands forward, aiming for the eyes. The blond's longer reach was ineffective at such close range, and Leopold managed to get one thumb in Dolph's right eye and he pushed hard. Dolph struggled to get away, but Leopold hooked his spare fingers inside the blond's ear and held him fast. He could feel the eyeball moving around under his thumb. He applied more pressure and Dolph screamed. The eyeball started to bulge from its socket. It was nearly out. He kept pressing and felt the tip of his thumb hit bone. Dolph kept screaming. Leopold kept pressing.

The giant soldier wrenched free and covered his face with his hands, blood oozing from the socket. He howled in agony, then launched himself at Leopold, fists flying in a frenzy. Leopold ducked the badly aimed blows and used Dolph's considerable momentum against him, shoving him onto the printing press, where he lay sprawled like a body on an operating table, jerking and writhing. His head was underneath the steel plate.

Leopold grabbed hold of the heavy screw handle above him with both hands and pulled. The screw drove the thick plate down onto Dolph's face, and Leopold used his full weight to force the mechanism tighter. He met resistance, but pulled harder and felt the plate start moving again. He heard a wet crack as Dolph's nasal bridge collapsed, sending blood and cartilage down the trapped soldier's throat. Leopold kept pulling. He felt more resistance as the plate met the trapped soldier's forehead and heard a muffled crunching sound as his skull began to give way. There was more blood and the cheek bones caved in. Dolph's body still jerked around, and Leopold kept pulling. There were several short, sharp snaps as the plate crushed Dolph's jaw bone and shattered his teeth; then he stopped moving. Leopold let go of the screw. Then he threw up.

"Leopold!" Mary's voice was strained. She and Jerome emerged from behind one of the bookcases and they both ran over. Mary caught sight of Dolph's mangled body and gagged.

The bodyguard nodded grimly. "Interesting improvisation."

"I'm lucky to be alive," panted Leopold. "Who knows what would have happened if they hadn't been distracted."

"I'm glad we didn't have to find out," said Mary, clutching her shoulder.

"What happened to you?"

"Nothing major," she replied, dropping her hand to her side. "Guy got a lucky hit in. Jerome had my back."

"He has a habit of doing that," said Leopold, wincing as the pain in his side intensified. "Jerome, do you have any painkillers in that first aid kit of yours?"

The bodyguard shook his head. "You'll be fine. I'd be more worried about all the damage we caused. What was it you said they kept up here? The entirety of human civilisation?"

Leopold sucked in a deep breath. "Nothing a few checks and a well placed donation won't cover. Maybe call in a few favors. We've gotten out of worse trouble before."

Jerome pulled out his cell phone. "I'll make the usual calls."

Chapter 34

Leopold found Albert lying face down on the floor with his hands clasped over the back of his head, whimpering quietly to himself. After a few shakes to the shoulder, Albert eventually got to his feet, where he stood shaking a little, but otherwise unharmed. The reading room was in tatters, with scraps of paper piled up like snow where high-velocity slugs had ripped through the thick volumes and sprayed their contents across the floor. The broken glass from the cabinets crunched under Leopold's feet as they made their way to the exit, and he felt his stomach lurch again as he caught a final glimpse of Dolph's mangled corpse.

They reached the deserted stair well and Jerome took the lead, checking for any signs of danger. He held up a two-way radio, snatched from one of the bodies in the reading room, and waited a few seconds. Silence.

"Looks like we're in the clear for now," said the bodyguard, slipping the radio into his coat pocket.

Jerome led them down the six flights of stairs to the ground floor, and Leopold noticed one of the emergency exits at street level had been wrenched open, most likely where Stark's men had entered. Jerome stuck his head through the disarmed emergency exit and waved them all through. They stepped out onto one of the narrow paths that wound behind the main university campus, sheltered on either side by carefully manicured bushes that stretched a dozen feet up into the air. The evening gloom had started to take hold and the light was fading fast, replaced by the muffled glare of the streetlamps that gave everything a slightly muted quality. A few seconds later, the bodyguard found the main gates and ushered everyone through to the main road, which was still lined with cars. Leopold spotted their battered SUV at the far corner.

"Nice car," said Albert, as they approached the vehicle. "Remind me not to go on any road trips with you guys."

Jerome took out the keys and unlocked the vehicle. Leopold reached for the handle to climb into the passenger seat but stopped suddenly, noticing a bright yellow clamp fixed to the front wheel and a parking ticket jammed under one of the front wipers. He swore loudly.

"Relax," said Albert. "It's not a problem. We can take my car."

Albert pointed to an ancient VW Beetle, straddling the curb on the opposite side of the road. The car was covered in dents and most of its paint had worn away, replaced largely by rust and scuff marks from decades of heavy use. Leopold and Jerome looked at each other.

"Are you kidding me?" said Jerome.

"What's the problem?" said Albert defensively.

The giant bodyguard shook his head and grunted, but didn't push the point any further. Leopold heard Mary chuckle quietly.

"We don't have much of a choice," said Leopold. "Forensics will have finished with Hank's apartment by now, which means Stark will be en route to clear up any loose ends before the detective teams get there."

"Let's get moving," said Mary, taking off in the direction of Albert's tiny car.

Leopold and Albert followed close behind, while Jerome loped after them with a reluctant expression. They reached the VW and the tour guide hopped into the driver's seat and buckled up. Leopold and Mary climbed in the back, knees pressed up against their bodies from the lack of space. Jerome paused at the door and frowned, then squeezed his massive frame into the passenger seat with a grunt of discomfort. The VW sank about six inches as he sat down, his shoulders hunched against the car's low roof. The bodyguard grunted again as he wrapped the seat belt around his contorted body and snapped it into place.

Albert started the engine with a metallic rattle and threw the manual gearbox into first with a disconcerting grinding noise, rolling the car out onto the road with a puff of black smoke from the exhaust. He wrenched the VW through various other gears as he sped up, trying to keep up with the other traffic as they merged onto the main road. The car struggled forward, eventually hitting its stride after a few minutes of spluttering from the old engine, and Albert breathed a sigh of relief.

Holding back a chuckle at the sight of Jerome squashed into the passenger seat, Leopold sat back as best he could and watched the traffic pass them on both sides. Mary pulled out her cell phone and made a call back to her office. Leopold didn't look forward to answering the awkward questions that were bound to follow once the NYPD discovered the mess they had left in the library. He caught Mary's eye and noticed she looked tired. She smiled as she noticed his gaze.

After nearly fifteen minutes the VW reached Hank's street. Jerome pointed to a parking space at the end of the street and Albert pulled up, hitting the curb with a muffled thump. Jerome wrenched himself out onto the sidewalk, followed closely by the others. The street was silent, other than the distant hum of the city traffic and the wind that whipped up the litter decorating the road. Leopold waited for the others to rearrange their crumpled clothes before setting off in the direction of Hank's apartment.

"Follow me. We don't have much time."

Leopold felt a crushing force hit him from behind and heard a loud *crack* as though the air above his head had just exploded. Jerome landed on Leopold, knocking him to the ground, followed shortly after by Mary and Albert, as the giant bodyguard grabbed the three of them and wrenched them toward one of the nearby alleyways, breaking off a nearby car's side mirror in the process.

The four of them toppled clumsily onto the ground. Mary slammed into one of several full garbage cans as a second *crack* reverberated, and part of the alley wall erupted in a cloud of dust and brick. Jerome forced his huge palms down onto Leopold and Mary's backs, forcing both of them to lie face-first on the ground, out of harm's way. Albert had rolled a little further down the passageway and was taking refuge behind one of the fallen garbage cans, underneath the fire escape that snaked its way up the wall.

"Keep down," growled Jerome. "We've got a shooter positioned a few buildings down. Caught the reflection of the street lamps on his scope."

"Is everyone okay?" asked Leopold, glancing around.

Albert squeaked in the affirmative. Mary didn't respond.

"She's out cold," said Jerome, leaning in close. "Doesn't look like any permanent damage."

The bodyguard assumed a crouching position, keeping the others behind him as he inched his way back toward the edge of the wall. He spotted the side view mirror that had broken away from one of the nearby cars lying on the floor, its glass still intact.

"Wait, don't do it," said Leopold. "It's too exposed."

"We don't have a choice," said Jerome, turning his head. "The alleyway behind us is blocked. If we stay here much longer the sniper will just relocate and pick us off."

Without waiting for a response, Jerome pulled off his coat and held it out into the street, in full view of the sniper. Another *crack* hit Leopold's eardrums as the jacket ripped in half, the bullet narrowly missing Jerome's fingers. Without wasting a millisecond, the bodyguard pushed forward and rolled out onto the street, scooping up the mirror and rolling back into the safety of the alleyway as another round narrowly missed the back of his head.

"There's no delay between the rounds hitting the wall and the sound of the shots," said Jerome, "so the shooter can't be that far away. Problem is, we can't hit back without knowing his exact position – which is where this comes in."

Jerome slid the mirror toward the edge of the wall and angled it at the far end of the street, in the direction of Hank's apartment but on the opposite side of the road. A second later, another bullet whipped past, catching the edge of the mirror and knocking it out of Jerome's hand. It landed a few feet away, useless. The bodyguard smiled.

"What the hell is there to smile about?" said Leopold.

"I caught the glare of his scope in the mirror. He's on the roof of the third building to the right, on the opposite side. This is good news, as long as he stays put."

"How do you know he will?"

"I don't. But chances are he won't move unless he absolutely has to. He's got us pinned down, so won't want to risk us escaping while he changes position. He's had a few near misses, so I'm guessing he's going to try his luck a few more times before switching on us. Here we go."

Leopold raised his hands in protest, but too late. Jerome moved with unbelievable speed and once again rolled out into the street, taking cover behind the parked car and drawing his Colt .45 as another *crack* rang out nearby. The car's back window exploded, showering the sidewalk with glass. Jerome took a deep breath and launched himself away from the car, firing three shots in quick succession as he ran, before diving back to his hiding place next to Leopold.

The bodyguard shook his head. "The angle wasn't right. We're going to have to get closer."

"What do you mean, *we*?" said Leopold, a sinking feeling clawing in his stomach.

"If I can get him to break cover, I can take him out."

"Let me guess. You want someone to draw fire? You know, this isn't typical procedure for a bodyguard."

"You'd rather Albert tried his luck?"

Leopold rolled his eyes. "Fine. What's the plan?"

"I need to get onto the roof here," said Jerome, slapping the wall. "When I give the signal, I need you to move back toward the SUV. When the shooter spots you and changes position to fire, I'll take him out from here."

"The SUV? He'll pick me off before I get anywhere close."

"There are enough parked cars to keep you covered," said Jerome. "If you move fast enough, you'll make it."

"And if you miss?"

"I won't."

Leopold opened his mouth to protest, but was too late. The bodyguard bounded toward one of the upright garbage cans and used it to launch himself high enough to catch hold of the fire escape that ran down the side of the apartment building. His fingertips caught hold and he used his momentum to grasp the bottom rung of the ladder with both hands. He swung his legs upwards and climbed to the lower platform. The rusty iron creaked under his weight as he ascended the metal staircase that led to the roof. As he approached the summit, Leopold saw him give the signal.

Pushing his nerves to the back of his mind, Leopold took a deep breath and shot out into the street, diving behind the damaged car that Jerome had used for cover earlier. Leopold closed his eyes and braced for the bullet, but none came. Relieved, he assumed a crouching position and prepared to make a dash for the next parked car, just a few feet away. He kept low and moved quickly, keeping his head out of sight.

He reached the next car and leaned up against the rear bumper. There had still been no sign of gunfire, meaning the shooter had either moved position or was waiting for a better shot. In either event, Leopold knew he would have to present an easier target to draw fire in his direction, allowing Jerome an opportunity to take the sniper out from the roof. A simple plan, but he knew that if the bodyguard missed, it was all over. The next bullet would be aimed directly at Leopold's chest, and he didn't fancy his chances of getting out of the way in time. Everything rested on Jerome's ability to make that one shot count.

Leopold screwed his eyes closed and bunched his fists. He counted to five silently and tensed the muscles in his legs, ready for his next move. Gritting his teeth, he rose to his feet and stepped into the middle of the road.

The sound of the gunshot was deafening, even from a distance. Leopold jumped in his skin and clutched at his chest, instinctively checking for blood. But there was none. The street fell silent and Leopold heard his heart thump against his rib cage, before realizing he hadn't taken a breath in nearly a minute. He exhaled deeply, relief flooding his body, and stumbled back to the alleyway, using the parked cars for much-needed support as he went. He rounded the corner as Jerome landed with a heavy thump, having jumped the ten feet from the fire escape to the ground.

"Did you take him out?" asked Leopold, leaning against the wall to give himself a chance to recover.

"I managed to catch the rifle and shatter the scope," said Jerome. "I think I may have wounded him, but he's still alive. I'll need to get closer to be sure."

Albert peeked out from behind his hiding place as Mary began to groan softly.

"Looks like she's awake," said Albert, kneeling down by her head. "I can make sure she's okay. You go ahead."

Leopold caught Jerome's arm as he walked past. "I'm going with you. You'll need backup in case there are any surprises."

He saw the bodyguard consider his words carefully, before nodding slowly.

"Fine. But you'll need to keep up."

Leopold nodded and followed him to the edge of the alleyway, both checking for any sign of movement in the street. When the coast was clear, Jerome counted down from three and they both sprinted as fast as they could manage in the direction of the shooter's position.

They reached the building in a matter of seconds, vaulting the fence and landing in the alleyway where the building's fire escape ran up the side wall. Jerome used a nearby dumpster to add height to his jump and grabbed hold of the railings, hoisting himself onto the rungs with relative ease. Stepping back a few feet to allow a running start, Leopold managed the same move and he hauled himself up onto the first set of stairs, struggling to catch his breath.

He reached the roof just a second after the Jerome, who drew his weapon as he surveyed the area. The roof was deserted. Other than the abandoned rifle and a handful of spent shells in the far corner, there was no evidence anyone had been there at all. A large air-conditioning unit sat square in the middle of the roof, making just enough noise to blank out the sound of distant traffic. Leopold kept his eyes on the unit as Jerome moved toward the broken rifle, his Colt .45 held in both hands.

Leopold saw the sniper attack as Jerome passed the air conditioning unit. The man wielded a short but lethal knife in his right hand, the blade angled away from his body to allow for a more effective attack to the throat. The bodyguard feigned surprise, which spurred his opponent's attack, but at the last minute he side-stepped out of the way.

The knife met only air as it narrowly whispered past Jerome's face. The shooter used the momentum of his failed attack to bring his left elbow around to catch the bodyguard's jaw, twisting his entire body to add extra force.

Leopold cringed as he waited for the blow to land, not knowing whether he should rush in to help, but Jerome was too quick and again sidestepped out of the way. As the sniper's body finished its rotation the two men were now face-to-face and square with each other. Jerome raised his handgun and squeezed the trigger, but the shooter dashed forward and parried the gun with his left forearm, angling his knife for an attack the throat.

Leopold saw Jerome drop the gun and bring his left arm up quickly under the shooter's wrist, pushing the knife harmlessly to the side. The sniper's momentum carried him forward and the bodyguard bent his right forearm to allow a clear path to the man's exposed throat. Jerome lunged and made contact with his fist, the combined force of their movements choking his opponent and opening up the chest area to further attack. He didn't waste any time and used his right fist to deal a powerful blow to the sniper's solar plexus while his left held the knife at bay.

As the shooter doubled over in pain, Leopold watched as Jerome brought the man's head down onto his knee, breaking the nose with a wet *crunch*. He wrenched the man's right hand away from his body, breaking the wrist with a sharp cracking noise.

Leopold held back a retch as he remembered the sound Dolph's skull had made as it shattered. Shaking his head to push away the memory, he ran over to join the bodyguard, who grabbed the sniper by the hair and pulled his head back.

"How many others are left?" growled Jerome, raising his fist over the man's exposed throat.

"Fuck you," the shooter gurgled, blood streaming from his ruined nose.

"Last chance. How many others are there?"

The sniper spat in the bodyguard's face and swore again. Jerome brought his right arm around the front of the sniper's throat and placed him in a choke hold. The man struggled, but could barely move under the force of the bodyguard's grip. He held the shooter's throat fast, increasing the pressure until Leopold saw him draw his last breath, his windpipe crushed under the fierce hold. Jerome felt for a pulse and found none. He let the body fall to the floor and walked back toward the fire escape, pausing long enough to let Leopold catch up.

Neither spoke a word as they made their way back to the alleyway below.

Chapter 35

When they reached Hank's apartment building the front door was open, wedged ajar by the decorators who were on their way out for the night. Leopold stood to the side to let them through and then slipped inside before the door closed, holding it open for Jerome, Mary, and Albert. The four of them made their way upstairs to Hank's apartment, where Mary pulled aside the police tape and stepped through into the living room.

Inside, the apartment had been swept thoroughly. Leopold noticed dozens of silver smudges on most of the surfaces, marking where forensics had taken fingerprint samples. Hank's body had been removed, but none of the blood had been cleaned up yet, pending results of routine DNA searches. Once the police confirmed the blood matches, no doubt they'd let the landlord clean up. It didn't look like the forensics team had gotten around to searching Hank's possessions yet. Probably left that to the detectives. Wherever they were.

"We've probably got a couple of hours till the detective team gets here," said Mary, absent-mindedly rubbing her head where she had knocked into the garbage cans. "The NYPD has quite a backlog right now, so they might be a while."

"Let's get what we need before anyone else shows up," said Leopold, stalking over to the bedroom.

He ruffled through the papers that had been left out on the desk and found the rest of the paperwork detailing Hank's banking transactions for the last month. He also found cell phone and Internet invoices, which he folded up and slipped into his jacket pocket. There was bound to be a link there somewhere.

"Did you find everything?" asked Mary

"Enough to get a warrant," said Leopold. "Then it's just a matter of time before we find a link to Senator Logan."

"What about Stark?"

"He's covered his tracks well. We can't even link him to the murders."

"But you proved they weren't suicides. The FBI knows someone set them up," said Mary.

"But they don't have enough to prove it was murder. Not beyond reasonable doubt. Even if they could, we don't have anything concrete linking back to Stark. That's what Stark was counting on."

"So what chance do we have?"

"Our only option is to catch up with Stark before anything happens to Christina. Then we'll have our proof."

Mary nodded grimly. "Speaking of proof, you still haven't explained how Stark managed to get in and out of a sealed apartment."

"Oh, that's easy. Follow me."

Leopold marched through to the kitchen and grabbed a large carving knife from the counter top. He walked back over toward the bedroom and stopped in the hallway. The others watched him from the bedroom.

"How does someone get in and out of a room without using the doors or the windows?" said Leopold.

The others shrugged.

"Simple. There's a way in and out that we haven't seen yet."

Leopold turned and brought the large knife down hard against the bare drywall behind him. He cut a rough circle and ripped out a hole about twelve inches in diameter. He could see straight through to the apartment next door, which was completely empty.

"Stark leases the apartment next door and cuts his way through to Hank's place. He waits for Hank to get home with Christina and kills him. Once he's done arranging the body he simply hangs a fresh sheet of drywall behind him and escapes with his hostage. With all the renovation work going on, nothing looks out of place."

"Why not just break down the door?" said Albert.

"Like I said, Stark makes his kills look self-inflicted. That way, if he's ever caught, a good lawyer can use reasonable doubt to acquit him of any charges."

"So what's our next move?" said Mary.

"Our only hope of finding Christina alive is catching Stark. If we make it in time, we'll have all the evidence we need to put Stark away for a long time."

"If we can find them in time," said Mary. "Where do we start to look?"

"Logan said he was coming back into the city this afternoon," said Leopold. "The most logical place to hold Christina is at Logan's town house, where nobody's going to walk in on them."

"The senator's not going to let them do that! He'd call the police the minute he suspected anything," said Mary.

"Senator Logan is dead," said Leopold. "No doubt about it."

A few seconds passed where nobody spoke. Albert shuffled uncomfortably and glanced around, presumably hoping someone would break the silence. Eventually, Mary obliged.

"Okay, let's say you're right."

"I am," said Leopold. "It was always Stark's intention to kill the senator, but it made sense for him to wait until he had a better idea of what was happening before making his move. The minute Stark sent his men after us back at the library, I knew the senator was dead."

"Okay, I believe you," said Mary hurriedly. "So we know where Christina is. And Stark. But how the hell do we get her out of there? The senator's place is going to be locked down. How do we get in? We won't get any support from the NYPD or the FBI without a warrant, which could take days. We don't have that long."

"Then we get her back ourselves," said Leopold.

"And how do we do that? We'll need a small army just to get through the door."

Leopold grinned. "I have an idea. Let's take a drive."

CHAPTER 36

The fluorescent lights that illuminated the windows of the high-class department stores and restaurants lining Fifth Avenue cut through the evening gloom as the VW Beetle rattled up to Leopold's apartment building. The sun had just begun to disappear beneath the skyline and the streets were getting a little quieter as most people were inside eating dinner, starting work on the night shift, or hitting the town for a few weekend drinks.

Leopold cringed as the car hit a pothole, feeling his teeth rattle in his skull. Albert pulled up to the building and entered the pass code into the keypad that opened the underground garage and the heavy gates opened up to let them through. The metallic knocking of the VW's old engine echoed loudly as Albert drove the car through to the reserved space at the back of the lot, closest to the elevators.

The four of them piled out and rode to the top floor, where Leopold punched in a six-digit pass code and the elevator opened silently into the penthouse apartment's cavernous entrance hall. The automatic lights came on and bathed the room with a warm glow. Albert whistled, clearly impressed.

Leopold led them through the enormous apartment, just as messy as he had left it earlier that morning, and opened a door that opened into a brightly lit room lined from top to bottom with glass-fronted storage cabinets. This particular room was unique in that it was meticulously neat. The cabinets were filled with laboratory equipment, and a large white counter filled most of the floor space, with a slim touchscreen monitor built into its surface.

"What's this place?" asked Mary, looking around with interest.

"Store room," said Leopold. "I keep most of my research equipment in here, but Jerome keeps some items in here too. Items I think we'll find useful."

Jerome stepped forward and entered a code into the touchscreen panel. A gentle whirring sound emanated from the unit and the entire countertop slid away, revealing a large storage cabinet underneath. Mounted to the interior walls were a dozen handguns, each of varying caliber, as well as hunting knives, throwing stars, and even a crossbow. In the center, on the floor of the unit, was a collection of chunky black objects that looked a lot like hockey pucks.

Mary turned to Leopold, hands on her hips. "I assume you have a licence for these weapons? They're not exactly *standard issue*."

"Of course," said Leopold. "And being a major shareholder of the country's biggest supplier of military weapons means I get access to some of the more interesting pieces."

"What are those things?" asked Mary, pointing at the hockey pucks.

"Anti-personnel explosives," said Jerome, before Leopold could answer. "Not as high-tech as the micro-explosives, but they pack a bigger punch."

"What kind of punch?" asked Albert, reaching out his hand to touch one.

Jerome grabbed his wrist and growled. "Enough to super-heat the blood in your veins to boiling point within ten seconds."

Albert gulped loudly.

Jerome reached his own hand out slowly, and picked up one of the explosives. "A simple twist of the casing and the explosive is armed," he continued, holding up the black disc. "The case is made from very low-friction alloy, so it slides easily across most surfaces toward your target's feet. A second or two later, and the device ignites, setting the target on fire rather than blowing him across the room. Makes for enhanced mayhem in confined spaces, with little impact damage to the surrounding area. Useful if you've got someone cornered."

"And why do we need to know this?" asked Mary.

"Like you said, we need the right tools to get to Christina. Take a look around; I think you'll find what we need," said Leopold, picking up one of the handguns and examining it.

As he held the weapon in his hands, he noticed a slight tremor in his grip and realized he hadn't eaten all day. He was hungry. Starving. "Show them the rest," he said, patting Jerome on the shoulder. "I'm going to fix us some dinner. It's not good attempting a daring rescue with low blood sugar."

Leopold left the others and went through to the kitchen. The automatic lights flicked on as he passed through, set for low ambient lighting at this time of the evening. The kitchen was modest compared to the rest of the apartment – which wasn't an issue for Leopold, who had most of his food delivered – but it still contained all the equipment needed to cook just about anything. The surfaces were reflective black marble and the appliances were finished with brushed aluminium and glass, except for the industrial-grade Viking gas oven which was stainless steel and took up most of the space.

Leopold opened the fridge and pulled out some cartons of leftover takeout from earlier in the week, stuffing them into the microwave in their containers. A few minutes later, the smell of Chinese food filled the room as Leopold emptied the contents of the cartons onto plates and laid them on the table.

The others soon came through, following the smell of food that had quickly filled the apartment. Albert was licking his lips. They sat at the large dining table overlooking Central Park and ate dinner just as the sun disappeared over the horizon. The city was a buzzing mass of floating lights, and the four of them ate hungrily without speaking, polishing off the meal in a little over five minutes. When they had all finished, Albert sat back in his chair and sighed contentedly.

"I needed that," said Albert, both hands resting on his stomach.

"Thanks, Leopold," said Mary.

"Good thinking," said Jerome. "We need to keep our energy up. No good getting dizzy in a fire fight."

Albert looked worried for a moment. Then a look of quiet contentment passed over his face and his eyes began to quiver. "Anything for dessert?" he asked, slurring his words slightly.

"What's wrong with him?" Mary asked, turning to Leopold.

"Don't worry. Just a little mild sedative I slipped into his food. It's more effective when injected, but it seems to have done the trick."

"What did you do that for?" asked Mary, sounding concerned.

"Like you said before, Albert's a civilian. He doesn't know what he's letting himself in for, no matter how eager he is to help. He'll wind up getting himself killed. It's a miracle he's still alive as it is; I'm not taking him along on this trip."

Albert tried to sit up, as though he couldn't hear what was being said. He gave up after a couple of unsuccessful attempts and resigned himself to the slumped position he had assumed in the chair. He put his hands back on his belly and slowly closed his eyes, breathing slowly and deeply. Then he burped and fell asleep.

"We'll put him in one of the guest bedrooms where he won't get into any trouble," said Leopold.

"So it's just the three of us against Stark's private army," said Mary. "Although I suppose that's more effective than the three of us plus Albert."

"What he lacks in skill, he makes up for in enthusiasm," said Jerome.

Mary cracked a smile. Leopold put his hand on her shoulder and felt her body move toward him slightly. She turned to look at him.

He looked into her eyes. "You need to be sure about this one, Mary. I don't want you there if you're in any doubt."

"Why would I be in any doubt?" she asked, blinking.

"You're NYPD. You've got due process and rules to follow. Chances are you'll get fired after this. Or worse."

"The way I figure it," she said, twisting herself away from him, "is that Christina's life is more important than my career, so I'll worry about the consequences later. No way I'm sitting this one out after everything I've been through today."

Leopold dropped his hand from her shoulder and nodded silently. The discussion was over.

"We've finished in the stores," said Jerome, breaking the silence. "I picked out a few items we can probably use. Of course, it would help to know the plan first."

Leopold stood up and walked over to the freezer. "Sure. I'll explain over ice cream."

Chapter 37

"That's your plan?" said Mary, glaring at Leopold as she spoke. "Are you crazy?"

Leopold, Mary, and Jerome were still clustered around the dining table, hand-drawn diagrams and maps covering the surface. It was nearly ten at night and tempers were beginning to fray.

"I don't see an alternative," said Jerome.

"Well of course *you* wouldn't, butler-boy," said Mary, pointing a finger at the startled bodyguard.

Jerome's expression darkened, and Leopold thought for a moment she might apologize. He was wrong.

"And don't give me that look," she continued. "I'm just trying to tell you where all the holes in your damn plan are. They're big enough to fall through."

Leopold sighed and tried to break the tension. "I know it's crazy, but it's the only plan we could even feasibly pull off in the time we've got. If we don't get Christina back by tomorrow, we'll lose her forever. We still have the element of surprise on our side; they won't expect an attack tonight from just three of us."

"Of course they won't," snapped Mary, "because that would be bat-shit crazy! How the hell do we storm a heavily fortified safe house, filled with armored super-soldiers, in the dark, with just the three of us? Don't you know *anyone* useful, with all your connections? We need backup."

Mary slapped both palms down onto the table as she finished speaking. Leopold jumped slightly.

"I'm afraid my professional network doesn't extend to hired mercenaries," replied Leopold, folding his arms. "Besides, we don't have the time to get a team together. Certainly not a team we can trust, at any rate. We're better off keeping this between us."

"It *will* work if we follow the plan to the letter," said Jerome, tapping the table with his index finger. "If we want to get Christina alive, it's our only chance. The only other viable option is to wait for a warrant, which will take too long. Do you have any better ideas?"

Mary didn't reply. She exhaled slowly and sat down, fingers locked in a pyramid, eyes closed. After a moment she opened her eyes and spoke. Her voice was calm again.

"What I don't understand, Leopold," she continued, "is what we're going to do if Stark has any more bleeding-edge weapons technology that we don't know about. It's bad enough going up against someone with a closet full of tiny bombs, without having to worry about running into some kind of space-age laser gun or something."

Leopold frowned. "It's unlikely he has access to anything else. The kind of technology required to get that much explosive power into something no bigger than a quarter takes some serious investment. Stark's a resourceful guy, but I doubt he's got access to that kind of money. I think he was given the micro-explosives to use for a very specific purpose."

"So, you're thinking he's not the one signing the paychecks?" said Jerome.

"I don't know," said Leopold. "All I can tell for sure is that his operation doesn't have anywhere near the resources needed to steal secret weapons technology from a secure military facility. Whatever he's got planned, it's going to be big."

Mary took a deep breath and let it out slowly. "Why don't you run your plan by me one more time?"

Leopold repeated his strategy and Mary listened. She and Jerome made a few suggestions, and Leopold amended some of the hand-drawn diagrams with busy scribbles as they spoke. After a few minutes they were all in agreement. This was never going to work.

But they were going to try anyway.

CHAPTER 38

The leafy Park Slopes suburb, nestled in an exclusive corner of Brooklyn, was a refuge for the rich and famous. The streets were immaculate and lined on either side with row after row of tall houses, set back from the sidewalk. Senator Logan's four-story townhouse was nestled in the center of the street, unremarkable from the outside and wedged between two identical-looking buildings. The house had a heavy wooden door at the top of a short flight of stone steps and huge windows blacked out with thick curtains. Were it not for the knowledge of what was inside, Leopold would not normally have given it a second glance. It was the perfect camouflage.

The streetlights emitted a soft glow, an altogether different light from the harsh neons of mid-town Manhattan, which would make it a little easier to avoid being spotted. This was an important factor. Leopold knew his plan would only work if they could access the garden at the back of Logan's house, which would inevitably mean climbing a few of his neighbors' fences.

Thankfully the lights were even dimmer at the end of the street, where Leopold could make out the wooden fence that marked the boundaries of the last house in the row. Once they had climbed over that, there were another six or seven fences to cover before they got to the right garden. From the satellite photos Leopold had printed out earlier, it would be easy to tell which was the right place; Logan looked like he'd spent a fortune turning his entire back yard into something that would give the botanical gardens a run for their money.

Jerome led the way, carrying a rucksack filled with the weapons they had picked out from the storage rooms earlier, and vaulted each of the fences with ease. Leopold and Mary followed, struggling to keep up.

"This is it," whispered Jerome, as the others landed on the soft grass of the largest garden and rolled into a crouching position.

Leopold held out his hands as Jerome unzipped the rucksack and handed out the equipment. The consultant had chosen a silenced Glock .45, which now felt a lot heavier in his hands than it had before. He looked around the garden, making mental note of blind spots and exit routes. He could make out an ornate gazebo nestled at the back of the plot, standing next to three large greenhouses filled with plants. To the front was an illuminated pond filled with what looked like carp. The rest of the expansive garden was thick with foliage, and the view of the house was obscured by bushes and trees. There was a good twenty feet of lawn, but there was plenty of cover around to reach the back door unseen. The real challenge was what they were going to do when they got there.

Leopold felt a cool splash on his face as the first few fat droplets of cold rain began to fall. After a few seconds, the intensity increased and he could hear the rainfall against the glass of the greenhouses, clattering loudly through the otherwise silent darkness. His eyes adjusted to the lack of light, and he could just about make out the silhouette of three cameras mounted at various points along the back wall of the house. There would probably be motion sensors and infra-red imaging too. There was no way they were getting anywhere near the house without Stark knowing about it. Fortunately, this was essential to the plan.

"We triggered the alarms when we landed," Jerome whispered. "They should send out a small team to investigate, just as we planned."

Leopold nodded and checked his watch. So far everything was running on time. He crouched next to Mary and stared intently at the back door, watching for any sign of activity. After a few seconds, the door opened and three armed men walked slowly out onto the flagstones, submachine guns raised at eye level. They wore armor but no helmets. Probably too dark. The weapons had torches mounted on them, and the beams cut across the garden, illuminating the heavy rain as it fell. Leopold watched the three men creep slowly and quietly deeper into the garden. He held his breath. They were only a few feet away from his hiding place.

The man at the front of the group raised his fist, signaling his companions to halt. The three of them kept their weapons raised, scanning the darkness for any sign of movement. Ten seconds of silence, then the leader relaxed his stance and lowered his weapon; the others followed suit. He reached for his radio.

PANIC

"This is Red Leader. False alarm. Probably a cat or something. No sign of any intruders. Coming back inside. Confirmation gamma-echo-delta-four. Over."

The radio fizzed and a voice on the other end acknowledged. The three men turned slowly and made their way back in the direction of the house.

Even though he knew it was coming, Leopold still flinched as Jerome fired his silenced handgun, the sharp *whip* sound making the hairs on the back of his neck stand straight up. He saw the bodyguard's shot catch the leader as his back was turned, piercing his skull as though it were soft fruit. Leopold and Mary followed suit, each taking out their target from behind with a single burst from their weapons, their silencers proving unnecessary as the mounting storm lashed about them. Their bullets slammed into the men's exposed heads and they crumpled to the ground like cut rope.

Jerome knelt and removed the leader's weapon and radio and Leopold and Mary did the same. As the bodyguard led the three of them toward the back door of the house, the consultant prayed the plan had worked. *Three go out, three come back in.* The infrared cameras wouldn't be able to tell the difference.

Leopold was familiar with the radio check-in procedures that most military units adopted. The last transmission had been a few seconds earlier, meaning they had anywhere between three and ten minutes before the unit commander would check on them again. When they didn't receive the right pass phrase over the radio, they would raise the alarm immediately and all hell would break loose.

The three of them slipped quietly through the back door and into the kitchen, taking care not to disturb the heavy frying pans and skillets that hung from hooks above the counter tops, and stood dripping near the back wall, checking for any signs of movement. The kitchen and dining area was large and empty, and appeared to be unused. Leopold could make out the other rooms from here, also empty, meaning they had this floor to themselves. Satisfied the coast was clear, Jerome signalled they could proceed, and Leopold pulled out the antipersonnel explosives from his backpack and placed them carefully on the counter top, taking care that they didn't slide off the polished surface. There were three in total, one each. The consultant handed them out as the radio in Jerome's hand stuttered.

"Red Leader, check in," a crackly voice came through the speaker. "Authenticate delta-alpha-delta-three. Over."

Jerome didn't answer.

"Red Leader, check in. Over," the voice came through again.

Jerome held the radio up to his mouth. "This is Red Leader, checking in. Over."

There was no response for a few seconds. "Roger that, Red Leader. Out."

"They know something's wrong," said Jerome. "We didn't have the code. They'll be sending a team to engage us. It's time to put the next phase of the plan into action."

"Take up your positions," said Leopold. "We only get one chance at this."

CHAPTER 39

The few lights in the house snapped into darkness. The soft glow that had given the rooms a warm and welcoming feel vanished in an instant, replaced instead by inky blackness and the occasional burst of white light from the storm flashing outside. The darkness gave more weight to the rain, which sounded like gravel hitting a tin roof. Leopold tightened his grip on the anti-personnel explosives and glanced over at Mary and Jerome, both stood ready for action, coiled up and tensed like springs.

Stark's men were using classic engagement tactics. First, kill the power and disorient your targets. Second, surround and cut off exit routes. Third, neutralize. Leopold knew the drill. He listened intently through the clattering of the rain for the sound of movement, but there was nothing. He glanced at Mary, who seemed to be thinking the same thing. Jerome kept still, tilting his head slightly, listening. There was only the noise of the storm outside as they waited in the stagnant darkness. Just waiting and listening. Finally Jerome's head turned sharply and he nodded to Leopold. They were here.

Leopold faced the doorway that led to the hall. Jerome and Mary covered the other entry points. Stark's men would attempt to surround them on each side, but they wouldn't be expecting a counterattack. They would expect a retreat. This single misapprehension would buy them a second or two to press their advantage, a fleeting chance of success. Christina's fate came down to how those two seconds were going to unfold.

They came like a battering ram. Like a stampeding herd. Two men at each door, six in total, bursting into the room with their heavy boots and submachine guns. Like their comrades, they wore body armor but no headgear. They moved in unison, a single entity with lethal intent. But they weren't expecting what happened next.

As the men entered, Leopold crouched and slipped out behind them before they had time to turn around to check their blind spots; a split second advantage brought about by the lack of light. Mary and Jerome did the same, and the three of them stood in separate doorways, looking in at the group of killers standing in the center of the room. The bodyguard nodded and each of them twisted the casing of their explosive, sliding them across the carpet as Stark's men turned to face them, weapons raised and ready to fire.

The grenades got there first. The white phosphorous and other chemicals inside the devices crushed together on detonation, sparking an exothermic reaction powerful enough to raise the temperature of the target area to five thousand degrees Fahrenheit. The room was lit up with a blinding flash as the phosphorous ignited, sticking to the clothes and skin of Stark's men. Leopold slammed the heavy door shut and dropped to the floor, avoiding the inevitable back-blast. He hit the ground hard, reigniting the pain in his ribs, just as the sprinkler system kicked in. Then the screaming started.

The white phosphorous was immune to the effects of the water pumping from the ceiling, and Leopold soon heard the *whoosh* of the white hot flames as they engulfed the room with astonishing speed and fury. He caught the acrid smell of melting fabric as the men's clothes melted onto their skin. The screaming got louder and the heat intensified as the flames grew, seeking more fuel. Those who hadn't passed out from the pain were still shrieking in agony as the blood in their veins reached boiling point and the last of the air was sucked out of their lungs by the hungry inferno.

Leopold gagged as the temperature near the door rose to an unbearable level, bringing with it the thick stink of chemical smoke and charred meat. The doors were modern and designed to resist fire, but it would only be a matter of time before the blaze got through. Hopefully they would hold out long enough for the flames to run out of fuel and die down, giving them just enough time to get to Christina before it was too late.

Stark was nine men down. With the mess at the library earlier, that brought the total dispatched to fourteen. The odds were getting a little better.

Chapter 40

Leopold sighed with relief as Jerome found the water supply to the house and shut off the supply to the sprinklers. The system cut out almost immediately, leaving the three of them drenched to the bone.

"Give me a minute and I'll try and get the power back on," said Jerome, stomping through the puddles that had formed on the floor towards a utilities cupboard at the far end of the kitchen. He pulled open the door and examined the circuit breaker panel within, settling on one of the larger switches and flicking it into position.

A split second later, Leopold heard a low thrumming noise and the lights flickered back on, forcing him to squint.

"How long do we have before the fire trucks get here?" asked Mary, her hair soaked flat to her forehead.

"This is an old system," said Jerome, closing the cupboard door. "The sprinklers are heat-activated, and work using a purely mechanical design, so it's unlikely they've been hooked up to alert the emergency services. I can't hear an alarm, so Stark has probably disabled it. Either way, nobody's on their way to help."

"Good," said Leopold. "If Stark sees sirens, he might panic. The fire doors should hold for now, we can call for help when this is all over."

"How can you know that?" asked Mary.

"The only way to completely extinguish white phosphorous is with sand or some other dry compound, which we don't have. Thankfully, the room is pretty well sealed, so there's not much air getting in. Without a steady supply of fresh air, the burn temperature will have fallen to a safer level. This gives us some time."

"How much time?"

"Impossible to tell. As long as no more air gets in, the phosphorous will eventually solidify and cool completely. We just have to hope nobody unseals the room, otherwise the fire will start up again."

"That's a great theory," said Mary, "but how about we get moving and put some distance between us?"

"My thoughts exactly," said Jerome, pacing through towards the staircase.

The bodyguard led the way up to the second floor, where the hard wood floors gave way to sodden carpet, which squelched noisily under Leopold's feet as he walked. He figured Stark would be holding Christina on the top floor, which would provide the most protection against an assault from ground level. Jerome checked his watch and nodded. The other mercenaries would know their attempt had failed by now, but the chances of another head-on assault were low. Stark's men would have to employ better tactics this time, which made them unpredictable. And dangerous.

Leopold stood at the rear of the group as Jerome led the way, treading carefully across the soaking wet carpet and stopping every few steps to listen for movement. It was almost as wet inside as it was outside in the storm. The sprinklers had blown most of the lights on this floor of the house, but it was still possible to make out gray shapes in the gloom, and the heavy rain had faltered a little so the house was quieter than before. He gripped his Glock .45 a little tighter.

Then the walls exploded. Leopold hit the floor, a split second after the others, covering his head with his hands and screwing his eyes shut as the bullets began to fly, ripping the walls and doors to shreds with a deafening volley of flying lead. He felt a searing flash in his shoulder as debris flew all around him, and opened his eyes to see a thick pool of blood forming where a large splinter of wood had lodged itself. He pulled out the fragment and tossed it to the floor, using a free hand to stem the bleeding. He glanced up at the spot where he had been standing, which had been reduced to a series of gaping holes, and tried to catch a glimpse of the others. As the dust from the ruined walls settled, he saw the outlines of Mary and Jerome. They were crawling flat to the ground, using their elbows for traction in an attempt to reach cover around the corner, where the corridor turned at ninety degrees and offered shelter. Leopold followed, and quickly realized they were being driven down a blind alley, with no escape route in sight.

As he rounded the corner and caught up to the others, he got to his feet, shaking slightly as he leaned against the wall, and caught his breath. Mary and Jerome stood a few feet away on the other side of the corridor, their breathing a little more controlled than his, but still audible above the noise of the rain outside. He heard footsteps approach from behind them, muffled by the thick carpet but still clear enough. A floorboard creaked, and then there was silence.

A small metallic object rolled into view, hitting the back wall with a soft *thump*. After a few seconds, smoke began to pour from it, curling upwards and quickly plunging the corridor into a choking cloud. Eyes stinging, Leopold stumbled forward and felt around with his arms outstretched, trying to catch hold of Jerome or Mary as he heard movement ahead.

He felt his breath knocked out of him as something hard connected with his gut, and he doubled over, coughing and wheezing, inhaling more of the sour-tasting smoke, and fell backward into one of the doors that lined the hallway. He wrenched at the handle and fell through onto the floor, kicking out with his feet and slamming the door shut. Something heavy collided with it on the other side and Leopold stood and pushed his entire body against the door, using his weight to keep it closed. The door shook on its hinges. He heard a crack as the frame splintered and the door fell through, knocking him backward with enough force to send him rolling across the floor. He collided with a coffee table, knocking his head against the heavy wood.

Leopold looked up, slightly dazed from the smoke and the impact of the fall, and looked around, trying to gauge his surroundings. He was lying on the floor of what looked like a study, but the lack of light made it difficult to tell. Thanks to the faint glow of the street lamps outside the window, he could just about make out a few tall book cases and a large desk, complete with an ornate high back chair that looked like it was worth a small fortune. Other than the coffee table he had just slammed into, the room was empty and, as far as he could tell, had only one door. There was no way out.

Leopold sucked in a deep breath and got to his knees as a shadow approached from outside the room. In the doorway stood one of Stark's men, surrounded by billowing smoke and wearing a gas mask. In the gloom he looked like a demon walking straight out of hell. Leopold blinked hard, getting the last of the smoke out of his eyes, and got to his feet.

The figure approached slowly, then stopped and pulled off his mask, revealing a maniacal grin and pockmarked face, visible even in the dim light. He stood at least a head taller than Leopold, who recognized the man's features immediately: Viktor, the unit commander who reported directly to Stark. Leopold clenched his fists and stood ready.

Viktor tossed his weapon onto the floor and cracked his knuckles. Leopold didn't wait for an invitation. He rushed forward and aimed a blow at the enormous man's side, connecting hard with the ribs. He hoped to crack at least one, but if his opponent felt anything he certainly didn't show it. Instead, Viktor reached out and grabbed Leopold's throat with two giant hands and squeezed. Under the impossibly strong grip, he felt his head begin to get hot and swell as the oxygen and blood flow to his brain was cut off. The commander's forearms were straining with the effort, the muscles wrapped together and tensed tight and thick like steel cable.

As the last reserves of his strength began to fade away, Leopold noticed the rims of his vision begin to darken, a vignette of red that signaled his optic nerves were beginning to fail. His pulse thumped in his ears like a muffled drum. *What a curious way to die.* Each system slowly shutting down, bit by bit, until there was nothing left. He felt a kind of peace at the inevitability of it all. It didn't even hurt any more.

Suddenly a cold rush of air flooded Leopold's throat and into his lungs. The relief was extraordinary. His vision sharpened again and the sound of his own heartbeat in his ears faded. He looked with curiosity at the man who wanted to kill him.

"I don't want you passing out too early," said Viktor.

Leopold couldn't speak, his throat was too swollen and raw. He looked into Viktor's eyes. They were small and black, but he could just make out a fleck of silver around the iris. It gave Viktor a bestial look, like some kind of creature that could see in the dark. Like a hunter. Leopold knew he wouldn't get another chance. As the feeling came back into his limbs, he felt his hands tingle behind his back and he began to unfasten the clasp of his watch.

"What's the matter? Nothing to say?" Viktor continued, pulling him closer. "Don't you have some clever plan to get you out of this one?"

Leopold sucked in another lungful of air and felt the throbbing in his throat ease a little. He managed a raspy whisper in response.

"What did you say?" said Viktor.

Leopold opened his mouth to repeat himself. "I said, I might have something up my sleeve."

The commander grinned and bared his yellow teeth. Leopold smiled back and unhooked the clasp from his watch with a quiet *click*, freeing the heavy, metallic piece from his wrist. With his other hand, he grasped the steel strap and brought his fist around quickly, aiming for Viktor's face.

The chunky watch acted like a set of brass knuckles, adding considerable force to his blow by concentrating the energy of the punch onto a smaller, harder surface area. As his fist connected with his opponent's cheek, Leopold felt bone crunch under the watch, which was reinforced with diamond glass, and gasped as white-hot pain flashed in his hand where his knuckles had absorbed the impact. Viktor let go of him and stumbled, reaching out with his huge hands to find support.

Leopold attacked again, but the giant soldier anticipated the move and blocked his attack without much effort. He whipped around, using his bulk to prevent escape, and lashed out with his right fist, catching Leopold in the solar plexus and knocking the wind out of him for a second time. He hit the floor hard, the impact painful enough to make him cry out as the thrumming pain in his knuckles reached a crescendo.

Leopold felt himself lifted to his feet again, as Viktor hoisted him off the ground. His vision swam as his opponent pulled him in close, his breath hot on Leopold's face. He attacked with his good hand, too fast for Viktor to block, and slammed his palm into the sneering commander's nose, crushing the cartilage. He wrenched himself free of his opponent's faltering grip and kicked out at his legs, hoping to catch the weak spot behind the knee.

Viktor must have anticipated the move. Instead of connecting with his target, Leopold's foot passed through empty air as the giant soldier moved out of the way and responded with a sharp jab to the side of the head. The blow hit home, and Leopold saw stars as he toppled back to the floor with the force of the impact, his body slamming hard into heavy wooden bookcase standing against the wall.

The shelves rocked unsteadily from the collision as Leopold shook his head and cleared his vision. His attacker advanced, surprisingly quick for his size, and brought down his heavy right boot, aiming for the face. In desperation, Leopold reached up above his head and fumbled for something he could use to protect himself. His hands grasped hold of something thick and heavy, and he whipped it forward to block Viktor's blow.

The soldier's foot connected with the hardcover edition of Leo Tolstoy's *War and Peace*, a massive tome that deflected most of the force of the attack to the side, knocking him off balance. Jumping to his feet, Leopold grasped the weighty book with both hands and lashed out at Viktor's face, slamming the front cover into the soldier's already broken nose. The commander howled in pain, before stumbling forward, fists raised and ready to strike.

Leopold dropped the cumbersome book and stepped backward, keeping his eyes fixed on his opponent's advance, until he reached the desk, where he was forced to stop. Pulse racing, he kept his gaze trained on Viktor, while his right hand moved down to his belt and he began to quietly unhook the metal buckle.

The attack came faster than he had expected, and Leopold moved too slowly to avoid Viktor's huge fist as it connected with his cheek. The force of the blow snapped his head to the side, disorienting him and causing him to stumble. He felt the commander's thick arm wrap around his neck once more, and he gasped in a deep breath of air while he still had the chance. As the soldier's grip intensified, Leopold again reached for his belt and finally got it free, gripping the expensive leather tight in his hand as he coaxed it out of the hoops in his waistband. With one final burst of effort, he whipped the belt at Viktor's face, sending the metal buckle hurtling toward the enormous man's exposed cheek. The heavy clasp hit home, hitting just below the eye with enough force to make the commander loosen his choke hold.

Fresh oxygen returned to Leopold's lungs, and he lashed out hard with his right leg as Viktor relaxed his grip, catching him at the knee and toppling the enormous man to the floor.

Viktor growled and got to his feet. He attacked wildly with both arms, blindly flailing in an attempt to land a lucky hit as one side of his face swelled and obscured his vision. He stepped forward and lashed out, but Leopold sidestepped him and aimed another kick to the back of his leg, forcing the commander to his knees. Leopold summoned the last of his strength and grabbed hold of the heavy desk chair, hoisting the ornate frame above his head before slamming it down hard on to the soldier's skull. The shock left his arms feeling numb.

Viktor crumpled to the floor and didn't move again. Leopold felt his forehead throb, suddenly dizzy. He sat down on the chair he had just used on Viktor. He was surprised it had survived the impact.

"Leopold!" shouted Mary, stepping through the doorway. "Are you okay?"

Leopold nodded but didn't speak. Jerome entered behind Mary and nodded in appreciation at Leopold's handiwork. The battered consultant groaned and got to his feet, stumbling slightly. Mary caught hold of his arm and steadied him. She looked worried.

"I'm fine," croaked Leopold. "Just a little dizzy. We need to keep moving."

Mary reluctantly agreed and helped him back out into the hallway, where he began to feel a little steadier. She let go and drew her gun. Jerome did the same.

"I didn't hear any shots," said Leopold. "What happened?"

"Jerome took his guy out pretty fast," Mary replied. "After that, it was two against one. No need for guns."

"Stark must be upstairs," said Leopold. "We need to take him out before he realizes he's outnumbered and does something desperate."

CHAPTER 41

The next floor was deserted, and Jerome swept through quickly, checking for traps. Nothing. Leopold kept his eyes wide open, now fully adjusted to the dark, and watched for any sign of movement. As they reached the next flight of stairs Leopold felt his pulse quicken. They were nearly there, just a few seconds away from Stark and Christina. The last set of stairs ended at a closed door, the master bedroom. A perfect place from which to run tactical operations and keep Christina close by. Jerome reached for the handle. It was locked.

Leopold heard a muffled voice, barely audible, coming from inside. It sounded like a woman's voice. Jerome shook the door but it wouldn't budge. He told the others to step back, and he used his shoulders to slam the frame, eventually crashing through the door on the third attempt.

The room was brightly lit and spanned the entire width of the house. The hardwood floors were littered with cables, surveillance equipment, two-way radios, and a myriad of other electronic equipment. There were large cupboards lining the walls, and pressed up against the bay window was a small desk littered with floor plans and blueprints of various buildings Leopold didn't recognize. At the far end of the room was a double closet. He could hear the muffled voice again.

Jerome seemed to hear it too, and crossed the room in a few long strides. He attempted to slide the closet door open, but it wouldn't budge.

"What's the problem?" asked Leopold, walking over.

"There's something behind here," replied the bodyguard, checking the seals around the panel with his finger tips. "Something that's supposed to stay hidden."

After a few seconds, Leopold heard a soft *clunk* as Jerome found a release catch, and the wooden panel slid into the wall, revealing a heavy, metallic door in the space where the closet should have been.

"What the hell is that?" asked Mary.

"Looks like a panic room," replied Jerome, rapping his knuckles against the metal. "Logan had a secret hideout up here. Guess he should have used it a little sooner."

"These things are quite common in my circles," commented Leopold. "Some of the wealthier home owners tend to be a little paranoid, so they have them installed. Most of them never get used."

"This one's been used – I can hear someone in there," said Mary. "It's got to be Christina. How are we supposed to get through?"

"It's nothing fancy, just a steel shell and a heavy door. These basic models only lock from the inside, so it was probably left open to allow Stark access."

"Good," said Jerome, pulling on the recessed handle. "I've seen enough modern technology in the last twenty four hours to last me a lifetime."

The bodyguard swung the heavy door open with little effort, and Leopold stepped forward into the darkness. Inside the fortified room, itself the size of a studio apartment, sat a young blonde woman bound to a steel chair. She was naked except for her underwear, which was stained with her blood and sweat. Her mouth was gagged with duct tape but her eyes were wide and alert, screaming out for help and welling with tears. Her skin was slick with perspiration and criss-crossed with cuts and scratches, as well as several deep gashes in her arms and legs that had been stitched up. She had clearly been tortured, then given medical treatment to stop her passing out from blood loss. Someone wanted to keep her awake.

Jerome untied her and knelt down on the floor. Leopold heard him ask whether her name was Christina, and she nodded weakly. The bodyguard gently removed the tape and helped her to her feet, putting his jacket around her.

"He isn't here," she said, her voice thin and quiet. "I heard him going downstairs. Then you came up."

Jerome turned to Leopold, who caught the worry in his eyes. "We must have passed right by him," said Jerome.

"Mary, check the stairs," said Leopold, turning to face her.

Mary stepped over to the broken door and peered into the gloom. Leopold heard her gasp, and Stark emerged from the doorway, one large hand on her shoulder and the other holding a gun to her head. He was standing behind her, using her body as cover.

"Don't move," said Stark, pressing the gun hard into Mary's temple.

Leopold stepped to the front slowly, hands up at shoulder-height, palms forward. "It's over Stark. There's nowhere to run."

He took another step forward, keeping Jerome and Christina behind him and out of harm's way. He caught the sound of thunder in the distance, as the storm outside intensified. Stark held his hostage tighter and pointed the gun at Leopold. Then he fired.

The bullet screamed into Leopold's shoulder, twirling him around and knocking him to the floor. The pain hadn't hit him yet. The bodyguard drew his own weapon, faster than Leopold could follow, and fired back, shoving Christina to the floor with his free hand. Stark cursed loudly and dropped his gun. Mary dropped to her knees and swiveled, aiming a punch at her attacker's groin, but he was too fast and landed his right boot heavily onto her face. She hit the ground and Stark rolled, avoiding Jerome's second shot.

Leopold caught his breath as the bodyguard crossed the room fast, making a direct line for Stark, who had picked up his gun and was on his feet. The two men brought their weapons around at the same time and fired, each dodging to the side just in time to avoid a bullet. Jerome recovered first and brought his firearm around for a second time, but his opponent caught his wrist and used the bodyguard's momentum to twist the gun out of his hand. Jerome kicked out and knocked

Stark's own weapon out of his grip. Both firearms were now on the floor, just out of reach.

Leopold blinked hard. His eyes were beginning to well with tears as the wall of pain hit him all at once. It felt like someone has twisted a superheated poker into his shoulder. If Stark got past Jerome, he wouldn't have the strength to defend himself. He looked on as the two huge men faced off. Both were a similar height and build, but Leopold hadn't seen the black ops colonel in action before and didn't know what to expect. His vision blurred and he began to feel faint. A damp pool of blood had formed on the floor where he had fallen, and Leopold reached for his shoulder in an attempt to stem the flow. As he put pressure on his wound, the agony intensified and sent shocks of white hot pain through his body, making him grunt with exhaustion as he tried not to cry out.

Jerome and Stark resumed their battle as Leopold spotted one of the handguns lying a few feet away. He forced the pain to the back of his mind and wrenched himself up on to his knees, wincing as his swollen knuckles protested and the pain in his ribs resurfaced. Eyes streaming, he forced himself to crawl in the direction of the fallen weapon, his progress agonizingly slow and clumsy.

"Leopold, get back!" shouted Jerome, recoiling from a vicious blow to the ribs.

Leopold flattened himself to the floorboards as Stark pushed the bodyguard backward into the wall and dove for the gun. The colonel rolled as he hit the floor, snatching the gun away before Leopold could reach it.

Jerome recovered fast, and hurtled across the room before Stark could bring the gun around properly, knocking the firearm out of his hand once again. The colonel snarled in frustration and lashed out with a roundhouse punch which landed hard to the bodyguard's jaw, knocking him off balance. Stark followed with a kick to the chest, landing squarely in the solar plexus, and sent Jerome crashing backward. He hit the wall hard and gasped for breath as his opponent came at him again.

Leopold swore under his breath as he realized the handgun was too far away for him to reach in his current state. The pain in his shoulder and ribs had become so intense he was having trouble concentrating. Without medical attention, he knew the loss of blood would make him pass out before much longer.

He struggled over to the edge of the room and leaned up against the wall, clutching his shoulder, and tried to focus on staying awake. Christina was lying a few feet away in the corner, knees up to her chest and head down. Leopold felt a momentary wave of relief as he saw her lift her face to look at him, before he turned his attention back to Stark and Jerome. If the bodyguard failed to protect them, Leopold knew they wouldn't last long. The sound of the storm outside grew louder as the heavy rain lashed against the roof like an endless hail of bullets.

Across the room, Stark slammed Jerome against the desk and aimed several blows to the ribs, throwing his punches with enough force to make the bodyguard tense his body in pain. Jerome adjusted his stance, grabbed his opponent by the collar, and pulled him forward, bringing his knee up fast to the stomach. Stark stumbled backward and Jerome tackled him, sending them both to the floor.

The bodyguard rolled away as they hit the floorboards and used the distance he had created between them to get to his feet and catch his breath. Stark followed, swaying slightly from the impact. Jerome charged again, lowering his shoulder and slamming the black ops colonel against the large bay window that overlooked the garden. The impact was enough to shatter the glass and frame, sending Stark toppling through the empty space to the ground below as the noise of the storm outside flooded into the room.

Leopold saw him disappear from view, sucked into the blackness, and heard two loud *thunks*, as Stark's body hit the roof and then the ground a few seconds later. Jerome peered out of the window before limping over to where Leopold lay on the floor.

"Stark's down," said the bodyguard, his breath heavy. "Can you walk?"

Leopold wasn't sure he could even breathe, let alone walk, as the pain in his shoulder peaked. It felt like his entire body was on fire, but he grunted and nodded anyway. Jerome helped him to his feet and turned to Christina.

"It's safe now," said Jerome. "You can come with us. We need to get you to a hospital."

Christina sat in the corner of the room, arms wrapped around her knees. She looked a second away from passing out, but nodded and took the bodyguard's free arm for support as she stood. As they made their way across the room, Leopold heard Mary groan as she regained consciousness.

"Where'd that bastard go?" said Mary. "I'm not finished with him yet."

Mary stood up shakily, swaying slightly, and noticed the broken window. She walked over and leant over the edge.

"So, where is he?" she asked.

Leopold grunted as he let go of Jerome and stumbled over to the window. He looked over the edge onto the garden below. The wind had picked up and was whipping the tree branches in a frenzy, casting contorted shadows over the grass where the streetlights cast their muted hue. The lawn was slick with rainfall, but empty. Stark had vanished.

"I heard him hit the ground," said Leopold. "Nobody could get up from that kind of fall."

"Stark's not a normal guy," said Jerome. "It take more than a short fall to stop someone like him."

Leopold saw Jerome register the panic in Christina's eyes.

"It's just a figure of speech," the bodyguard added, quickly. "He's not coming back any time soon, don't worry."

"You're safe now," said Mary. "The police and ambulance are on their way. We'll make sure you're looked after, don't worry."

Christina smiled weakly and held on to Jerome's arm as they walked, while Mary located her cell phone and called her precinct' dispatch team direct. Leopold eventually managed to stumble downstairs with minimal help from Jerome, wincing in pain at each step.

As they reached the kitchen, the sound of sirens cut through the howl of the storm outside, and Leopold sat down in the dining room to wait for the medical team to arrive. He felt the last reserves of his energy seep out of his body as he settled into the cushion; and he closed his eyes, letting the darkness and pain wash over him.

Chapter 42

Leopold knew he was about to wake up when he dreamed that he was dreaming. He understood that he was lying on a bed, that he was on his back and that he couldn't move. For what seemed like days he had slept in a state of near-consciousness, dreams flickering in and out in a procession of terrifying scenes and painful memories. He did nothing to disturb them, made no effort to stir until the sound of a familiar voice washed over him.

"Leopold? It's time to wake up now."

He knew Mary's voice. It always surprised him how soft she could be at times. He pushed the thoughts out of his mind and concentrated instead on pulling himself back to the waking world. He felt his eyes slowly grind open – they felt a little stuck – and then the light hit him.

He was in the hospital; that much was obvious. He was in a private room, but he wasn't alone; there were four other people there. Leopold squinted and the room came back into focus. Standing beside his bed were Mary, Jerome, and Christina. At the other end of the room, inspecting the contents of the bookshelves, was

Albert. He turned and grinned before bounding over to the bed.

"Leopold! Thank God you're okay. You had us worried there for a moment!" said Albert, practically bouncing up and down.

"Speak for yourself," said Mary, smiling. "I knew he was tougher than he was making out. All those tears were just for dramatic effect."

"Good to have you back," said Jerome, his face as imperceptible as ever.

Leopold grunted and sat up in the bed, wincing slightly as he felt his shoulder. The pain was subdued, but most definitely there.

"The doctors stitched you up," said Jerome. "The bullet went straight through and didn't catch the bone, so there shouldn't be any complications."

Leopold nodded and looked over at Christina. She was wearing a hospital nightgown that covered her arms and legs. She smiled back at him, but it was forced.

"Don't worry, I'm fine," said Christina. "At least physically, anyway. Jerome told me about my dad."

Judging by the redness of her eyes, she had been crying for a long time.

"The doctors said my injuries were only superficial," she continued. "They said the cuts were clean and the stitching was professional, so they decided to leave them alone. Just gave me some painkillers. They said I had traces of morphine in my system, so they couldn't give me anything stronger. Still itches like hell, though."

She rubbed her arm absent-mindedly. "I have to check out today, so I wanted to come by and say thank you. You know, for everything. For getting me out of that… place."

"Are you sure you have to leave today?" asked Mary, putting her hand on Christina's shoulder.

"Yes, I'm sure. It's my father's funeral this afternoon and I have to be there. I'm sure you understand."

Mary nodded and smiled sympathetically. Christina thanked her and turned to Jerome.

"And thank you for everything you've done, too. I know I wouldn't be alive today if it weren't for you. For all of you."

The bodyguard mumbled something in reply, and Christina left the room, as more tears began to well in her eyes.

"How long have I been in here?" asked Leopold.

"Two days," replied Jerome. "You lost quite a lot of blood."

"And Stark?"

"Nowhere to be found. He got away."

Leopold frowned and lay back down in the bed. They had been so close. No matter, they had Christina back, which was all that really counted in the end. He knew she would be okay, eventually. If the details of Senator Logan's corruption ever went public, they would no doubt be covered up by his estate. It was pretty easy to get a gag order when your family knew all the judges. No point in fighting them. Let the authorities finish the job.

Leopold relaxed a little at the thought of handing this case back. He had found Christina, which was what he was being paid for. He would give the FBI everything they needed to link Stark to the murders, and give them

Logan and the charity scammers on a silver platter. All that was left to do now was rest and recover.

"Are you well enough to go home?" asked Mary.

"Yes, I think so. Jerome, can you bring the car? I'll handle the paperwork."

Jerome nodded and left the room.

"I suppose you'll be getting back the precinct now?" asked Leopold.

"Yes. I think my boss is finally going to be off my ass now we've managed to give the FBI something. Hopefully this will keep him happy for a while. I don't think I can manage too many more graveyard shifts."

Mary leaned over and kissed him softly on the cheek, and then walked out the door, leaving Leopold and Albert alone in the room.

"Albert, I'm sorry about everything that's happened. We should never have gotten you involved."

"Are you kidding? The last few days have been the most fun I've had in of my whole life. I used to spend all my time indoors sitting at a computer, and now I actually have something interesting to tell my kids one day! If I ever have kids. I bet I will, though. The ladies love an action hero."

Leopold smiled and held out his hand. Albert shook it vigorously.

"Thank you. If you ever need anything, *anything*, just let me know."

"How about not shaking me so hard?" replied the consultant, grimacing. "Stitches, remember?"

"Oh, sorry."

He let go and bowed awkwardly instead, making Leopold laugh out loud. Albert grinned again and left the room, closing the door behind him quietly. The consultant lay in the quiet room alone and exhaled deeply, feeling the pain in his shoulder start to recede once more. He closed his eyes and drifted off into a dreamless sleep.

Chapter 43

Jerome picked him up from the hospital in the '66 Shelby Cobra, and Leopold listened to the eager growl of the huge V8 engine as they rode through town. Not as comfortable as the Mulsanne, which was scrap metal by now, but more exciting than the town car gathering dust in the garage. Leopold figured Jerome wanted to blow off steam.

At the apartment, the consultant went straight into the living room and slumped in one of the armchairs near the fireplace, grabbing the bottle of scotch from the coffee table and pouring himself a healthy slug. The liquor hit the back of his throat and he closed his eyes, feeling the heat of the alcohol swell in his chest. He turned on the television and flicked over to the news channel, hoping to find out whether the last few days had hit the headlines yet. He didn't have to wait long.

Jerome brought over coffee and they both sat and watched. The newsreader was touching his ear as the breaking news came in. They cut to a video of Christina, dressed in black, getting out of a polished limousine at one of the city's many cemeteries, surrounded by journalists and reporters. She looked dazed and exhausted. Several reporters jabbed oversized microphones in her direction, but she kept her head down and pushed through. Leopold hadn't expected such a large crowd.

The news anchor was back again and was talking excitedly, reporting that they had just received official confirmation that the President of the United States would attend the funeral. Leopold sat up in his chair.

The video feed switched to a hastily compiled video montage, displaying photographs of the President and Senator Logan together at various public and private events over the years. The news anchor mentioned that the two men had been good friends and that the President always took the time to honor his friends and loved ones. The news anchor was laying it on a little thick. Election year.

A black-and-white photograph of the Commander in Chief and Senator Logan shaking hands filled the screen as the anchor spoke. In the picture, the number fifty-three hung in an enormous banner behind the two men, and there was a half-eaten cake with candles on a large table in the foreground. It was the same photograph Leopold had seen nearly three days ago at the senator's house. The same photograph Stark had apparently been so interested in.

Realization abruptly shot through Blake's tired mind. "Jerome, fetch the car," said Leopold, getting to his feet. "We've got about twenty minutes to get to that funeral before we have two more dead bodies on our hands."

CHAPTER 44

Jack Stark crouched atop the hill, his position covered by the thick foliage that grew around the private mausoleum, and peered through his binoculars. He was dressed in combat fatigues, the camouflage pattern perfectly blended in to his surroundings. The colonel opened the pack he had carried up with him and pulled out his rifle, an M99 Barrett with a custom scope. The rifle was high-caliber and designed for longer range work, but it was still just as effective at shorter ranges.

The Barrett used solid brass rounds and propelled them at three times the speed of sound, keeping the bullets supersonic for nearly a mile and a half. Stark didn't need to worry about range or being spotted; at this distance, the round would hit its target a full second before the soundwaves did, so a silencer wouldn't be necessary. More accurate that way.

The rifle itself was made from matte black steel and was around fifty inches in length when assembled, most of that length in the barrel. The weapon was single-shot bolt-action, which made for greater accuracy and reliability than a semi-automatic but resulted in a delay while the next round was loaded into the chamber. No matter, there was only one target Stark cared about, and the mechanics of a bolt-action were somehow more satisfying. More brutal. Stark smiled at the thought.

He pulled out the bipod, barrel, trigger assembly, bolt assembly, and butt plate and carefully assembled the weapon, securing it in place. He lifted the weapon and positioned himself near the edge of the bushes, where he set the rifle down so that the muzzle just protruded from the leaves, still partially obscured from sight. He rested his right elbow on the soil and squeezed the trigger with his index finger. The empty Barrett responded with a satisfying deep metallic *thunk* resonating from the breech.

Stark took out a single round and loaded it into the chamber, secured the bolt in place, and placed five more on the ground to his right, tips facing up. He attached the rifle scope, flipped open the lens cap, and looked through the sight. He adjusted the scope to his requirements and replaced the cover. He smiled with satisfaction. The perfect killing tool. And if the plan went as it was supposed to, he wouldn't even need to fire it.

Chapter 45

The Shelby Cobra screamed out of the garage and tore down the street, wheels spinning furiously in an attempt to gain traction and put the engine's five-hundred horsepower to good use. Jerome sat in the driver's seat, his right foot planted to the floor.

"Are you going to tell me what this is all about?" said the bodyguard, not taking his eyes off the road as they barreled forward, the tires finding the grip they needed.

"The President," said Leopold. "That was Stark's target all along. Stark knew the senator and he were close, and knew that the President would be at the funeral."

"How's he going to take out the President in a public place? He'll never get close enough."

"Think about Christina's injuries. Why would someone cut into a person's flesh, only to stitch it up again? The doctor said that there were traces of morphine in her system, that she wouldn't have felt a thing the whole time. The cuts weren't torture."

"So what were they?" asked Jerome, shifting gear as they rounded a corner.

"It first caught my attention when she said the cuts were irritating her," said Leopold. "I could see the swelling when we first found her, but assumed it was an infection. The only other thing that would cause a reaction like that would be a foreign body, placed underneath the skin."

"Let me guess – like micro-explosives?"

"Exactly. Judging by the number of deeper cuts, Christina could have as many as six explosives implanted underneath her skin. All Stark has to do is wait for her to get within a few feet of the President, and then trigger the detonator. The blast would be strong enough to vaporize both of them," said Leopold.

"Stark could pull that off from a distance with a cell phone. All he'd need would be a clear line of sight to keep an eye on his target."

"Yes. Which means he has to be at the cemetery. We need to get there before the President arrives and gets too close to Christina."

"Can't you call this in?" asked Jerome, his eyes fixed on the road ahead.

"And who's going to believe me? By the time I get through to the right people and convince them I'm not some wacko, it'll be too late."

"Fair point", replied Jerome. "Looks like we're on our own. I'll need directions."

"The funeral is at Green-Wood Cemetery," said Leopold, his voice raised over the noise of the engine. "That's in Brooklyn. Must be a family plot or something, seeing as they stopped taking bodies years ago. Nothing the right connections can't fix.

"It's at least thirty minutes in this traffic."

"We don't have much of a choice. Just floor it."

The bodyguard smiled and revved the engine to five-thousand rpm. He shifted down from fifth gear to third and the Cobra surged forward, reaching seventy miles per hour within two seconds. Leopold felt the force of the acceleration slam him into the back of his seat as Jerome crossed over into the bus lane and the slow NYC traffic fell behind.

Ahead, a public bus pulled out onto the road, coming up quick. The bodyguard swore and wrenched the wheel to the left, merging with the rest of the traffic and narrowly avoiding a blue pickup that was a few feet behind them. The driver of the pickup sounded the horn angrily and Jerome swerved back into the empty lane with a screech of rubber as they flew past the bus, escaping a rear collision with a white SUV ahead. As they cruised ahead, Leopold turned and saw the driver of the SUV stare at them, slack-jawed. He waved back, cheerily.

He flicked on the radio and eventually found a station reporting on the funeral details. The reception was fuzzy, but he could just about make out the news reporter over the static. The President was on his way and due to show up in less then ten minutes. Jerome gripped the wheel tighter and kept his right foot down.

After a couple of minutes they reached Manhattan Bridge, a two-lane highway that spanned the Hudson river and connected Manhattan Island with Brooklyn. The traffic ground to a halt at the intersection, forcing Jerome to slam the brakes. From where they sat, Leopold could make out a line of cars spanning the entire bridge, none of which was moving.

The bodyguard swore again and pulled out onto a pedestrian crossing, forcing several bystanders to jump out of the way. From here, Leopold could see that one of the bridge's lanes was closed due to maintenance, marked by a line of orange traffic cones.

"Hold on," said Jerome.

Jerome revved the engine again and released the clutch, sending the car hurtling forward in a cloud of burnt rubber. The traffic cones were scattered to the side as they surged forward, bouncing off the bodywork of the vehicles lined up in the other lane.

"I don't see any holes in the road," said Jerome.

"They usually close off one of the lanes to keep the maintenance guys safe while they work on the support systems."

"Good. I wasn't looking forward to what might happen if there were any chunks missing out of the bridge."

Leopold grinned in agreement. Hitting so much as a pothole at this speed would wreck the suspension send them spinning out of control. The radio cracked again. The President had arrived.

Jerome urged the car forward, squeezing every last drop of speed out of the giant engine. As they crossed the halfway point, Leopold spotted a flash of blue light reflected in the rear-view mirror, followed shortly by the sound of a police siren.

"Dammit, looks like we've attracted too much attention," said Leopold, glancing back in his seat.

The flashing blue lights of the police car stayed reassuringly far behind as they sailed over the Manhattan Bridge. As they entered Brooklyn, the traffic began to merge into both lanes again and Jerome had to swerve to avoid a collision. He turned onto the expressway and put his right foot to the floor, passing the other cars and sweeping from lane to lane to avoid the vehicles in front.

The blue lights were getting closer now. Leopold knew the patrol car would have radioed ahead for backup by now, but there wasn't much anyone could do to them while they stayed on the expressway, other than track their progress. Once they hit the suburbs, things would be a little more challenging. The radio announced that the President's car was pulling up. They weren't going to make it.

Jerome didn't slow down as they hit the exit for Green-Wood, swerving the car in a tight turn onto Third Avenue and into the rough industrial areas that surrounded the picturesque cemetery. The blue lights of the police car had vanished now, lost in the maze of streets and bustling traffic, but Leopold knew there would be more waiting.

As the Cobra charged down Twentieth Street, the grassy mounds of the Green-Wood cemetery rolled into view, peaking above the black iron fence that rose ten feet or so above the sidewalk and wrapped around the entire park. The lawns were littered with headstones, most of which were old and crumbling, and the swaying branches of oak trees were visible in the distance. Christina would be toward the center of the cemetery somewhere, where the expensive plots were kept. The radio presenter announced that the President was getting out of his car.

Jerome wrenched the car onto Fifth Avenue with a shriek of spinning rubber and executed a wide turn without dropping the engine speed, fishtailing slightly as he span the steering wheel to compensate. The entrance gates to the cemetery were close by. That's when Leopold saw them coming.

Ahead, not more than fifteen hundred feet, a strip of flashing blue lights rushed toward them. The sirens cut through the noise of the traffic, a cacophony of high-pitched wails that bounced off all the buildings around them. Leopold saw the three squad cars screech to a halt and half a dozen police officers spill out onto the street, dragging a heavy chain of traffic spikes across the road behind them, before taking up positions behind their vehicles. The spikes were between the Cobra and the entrance gates, and there was no way to avoid them.

"We have to keep going," said Leopold. "We won't make it on foot. Hopefully the wheels will hold out long enough to get us within range. If we're lucky, the Secret Service will get the President to safety as soon as they see us coming."

"And if they don't, how close do you need to get?"

"I need to be within fifty feet of Christina to block the explosives' ability to receive a signal. I'll get the program ready now; pass me your cell phone. I'll need to keep mine as a backup."

Jerome handed over his cell phone, and Leopold activated the same program they had used to gain access to the Columbia computer networks. The phone would broadcast a scramble signal that would block any wireless transmissions within a fifty-foot radius, including the detonation signal that Stark would try to send. As long as the cell phone had power and Leopold could get close enough, the colonel wouldn't be able to trigger an explosion.

The Cobra approached the traffic spikes and Jerome slowed down slightly. The police officers held fast behind their vehicles, handguns drawn. Leopold braced for impact. The Cobra hit the spikes at fifty miles per hour, and he heard the loud *pop* as the front tires were shredded, followed by another *pop* as the rear set were torn apart. The car veered from side to side as they lost traction and Jerome just managed to keep them out of a spin. They were just a few meters from the gates now, and the bodyguard put the car into a low gear and urged the car forward, sending sparks flying from the bare wheels beneath them. The sound of screeching metal was all Leopold could hear as the rims struggled to grip the asphalt.

He watched as Jerome wrenched the steering wheel sharply to the left and right, giving the wheels some extra grip, and the Cobra lurched forward, grinding its way toward the heavy metal gates that led into the cemetery. The speedometer reluctantly hit twenty miles an hour, and the bodyguard coaxed the crippled speedster down the wide paths that led into the center of the park, leaving the bewildered police officers behind. Thanks to the number of pedestrians in the area, Leopold knew it was unlikely the authorities would follow by car. That would at least buy them some time.

Less than a minute later, they pulled up near to a large crowd of mourners, all dressed in dark colors and standing with their backs to the road. The sea of people was huge, and their attention seemed to be focused elsewhere, so nobody noticed the battered Cobra approach, screeching to a standstill just a few dozen feet away from the edge of the congregation.

A few town cars were parked nearby and Leopold could see that one of them carried the flag with the Presidential seal. He looked around for any sign of disruption, and his heart leapt as he realized they might not be too late. They both flew out of the car and ran into the mass of people, pushing their way through the throng in an attempt to reach the procession in the center of the crowd.

Leopold took the lead and finally caught a glimpse of the casket, carried on the shoulders of the pallbearers a hundred feet ahead. A few seconds more, and he could make out Christina, sat close by and holding a large bouquet of white flowers. Just a little further, and he could see the President walking slowly toward her. He sat down on an empty chair and put one hand on her shoulder. This was the moment that Stark would be waiting for.

They were still too far away, out of range of the scrambler. Leopold made one final, desperate attempt to claw his way through the thickening crowd. No use. He took the cell phone out of his jacket pocket and hurled it forward, praying it would land within range. That's when he heard the explosion.

Chapter 46

Everyone hit the ground. Leopold covered his head with his hands and screwed up his eyes, lying face-down on the lawn. They were too late. Just a few seconds earlier and everything would have been all right. Now he knew Christina was dead, and the leader of the most powerful nation on Earth was just a corpse on the grass. Snuffed out in an instant.

The ringing in Leopold's ears faded. He slowly opened his eyes and looked around. At least two hundred people were sprawled on the grass, many of whom began to lift their heads and look around. Nobody appeared to be shouting or screaming. Three black-suited men were sprinting toward him from the direction of the President, who was also lying on the floor a good twenty feet away from Christina and surrounded by bodyguards. He was breathing.

Leopold turned his head and looked behind him, confused. Jerome was standing tall, his gun in his hand and pointed at the sky. The barrel was smoking. As Leopold realized what had happened, Jerome was tackled at full speed by the black-suited men, who wrestled him to the ground and pulled his weapon off him. As he went down, Jerome caught Leopold's eye and winked. He had provided Leopold with the perfect diversion and now the President was out of harm's way, separated from Christina by his Secret Service bodyguards and out of range of the explosives.

Leopold turned his attention back to the President, who was getting to his feet, and realised that the men who had brought down Jerome had left the Commander in Chief exposed, with only two security officers now remaining by his side. The pair of towering bodyguards seemed to have the same concerns, as they edged in closer to each other while ushering their charge toward the town cars.

They neared the safety of the vehicles, and the taller officer was suddenly thrown backward. A spray of crimson erupted from his shoulder as he fell, and what sounded like a thunderclap echoed across the park. The wounded bodyguard hit the floor hard and stayed down. The other dived on top of the President, knocking him to the ground and rolling them both behind the President's town car and out of harm's way. Two of the men who had wrestled Jerome to the floor joined them and took up defensive positions behind the vehicle, handguns drawn.

It looked like Stark was reverting to plan B.

Leopold got to his feet and ran toward Christina, his path clear now that everyone was down on the grass, and grabbed his cell phone from the ground as he passed. He reached her and thrust the device into her hands.

"Keep this turned on and with you at all times," he said hurriedly, "it will keep you safe."

"Safe? Safe from what? What's going on?" said Christina.

"Your injuries. Stark implanted explosives under your skin. This cell phone will jam the detonator. I have to go find him."

Her eyes widened in horror as the consultant's words hit home and she stared in revulsion at the raw scars on her exposed skin. Quickly, she pulled herself together.

"He's here? You can't go after him alone. You know what he's capable of."

"There's no time to explain to the Secret Service. Even if they don't shoot me, by the time they realise I'm not a threat, Stark will be long gone."

"But he's got a rifle – you'll be killed," said Christina, eyes wide and imploring.

"He's not going to stick around, not now the President is safe. He had his chance, and he blew it; retreat is the only option. By the time he shoots his way through the Secret Service, the police will be here."

"This place is huge. How can you expect to find him?"

"There's only one vantage point with a direct line of sight within range. The sound of the shot came less than a second after the bullet hit its target, which puts Stark not more than about a thousand feet away. If I were him, I'd be up there."

He pointed at a white marble mausoleum standing atop a set of steps that ascended a small hill in the mid-distance. The mausoleum was sheltered by thick trees and bushes stretching out almost the entire width of the park on each side. It was the only possible place Stark could get a good view of the funeral procession anywhere within range. Before Christina could say anything to stop him, Leopold sprinted in the direction of the steps, hoping that Stark hadn't decided to stick around and pick off anyone coming after him.

He reached the top of the steps in less than a minute and paused to catch his breath, scanning the surrounding area. Walking slowly toward the entrance to the mausoleum, he noticed boot prints in the grass. Stark had definitely been here.

He heard a faint rustle to the right, coming from somewhere inside the long strip of trees that ran most of the width of the park. The cover was dense enough to hide anyone wanting to get in and out of the cemetery without being seen. Leopold ran into the trees, cursing himself for not bringing a gun and hoping that Jerome managed to convince the Secret Service he was on their side.

Fifty feet in, the cover of leaves blocked out most of the direct sunlight, except for the occasional ripple that made its way through to the dry ground. Other than this, the dense undergrowth was dark enough that Leopold couldn't make out a clear path, and he had to slow his pace. He heard another rustle ahead of him, louder this time, and he crouched, ready to defend himself.

The cover of leaves burst open as a dark figure shot out and knocked him to the ground. Within a second he was back on his feet, just in time to see a large dog disappear around the corner, dragging its leash along behind. False alarm. Stark was probably long gone by now.

Leopold wheeled around as he heard twigs snapping behind him, expecting to get knocked to the ground by whatever animal had decided to make a quick exit in his direction. Instead, the consultant met the savage gaze of Jack Stark, his face set in frustration and fury. The colonel was dressed in full camouflage, with a rifle case strapped to his back and a handgun holstered to his belt. Leopold heard his pulse throb in his ears again and he tensed his muscles, ready to defend himself. He had to keep Stark occupied long enough for Jerome to convince the Secret Service to get up here and take him down. Leopold hoped he could last that long.

Stark crossed the distance between them in a single step and caught hold of Leopold, pulling him close. The consultant knew he was outclassed. This was a man who could hold his own against Jerome, and that was something he had never seen before. He didn't stand a chance. But maybe, just maybe, he could hold him off long enough. Leopold's brain was still spinning when Stark hit him, the force of the blow landing like a freight train. The spark of hope that he had kept in the back of his mind vanished immediately, as he realised he wasn't going to make it out alive.

Chapter 47

Leopold felt his brain turn in his skull as the force of Stark's punch wrenched his head to the side and blanked out his vision. He felt himself hit the ground just before his eyesight came back again, and the first thing he saw was his opponent's heavy right boot fly toward him, slamming into his side. The impact knocked him on his back and he heard something snap. Probably another rib.

He gasped as he landed and tried to roll away, but Stark aimed another kick at his back. The blow landed hard to his shoulder and Leopold was on his front again. He managed to get up onto one knee and look up at his attacker, who was grinning. All the cold, calculating, demeanor had vanished, replaced with a look that was almost gleeful. Leopold knew the look of revenge when he saw it. The colonel pulled out his handgun.

The fight was over. Leopold knew it. But he just had to hold on a little longer, just enough to let Jerome find his tracks and get the Secret Service up here. He got to his feet, swaying slightly as he stood. He raised his fists. Stark laughed.

"I was going to make this quick," said Stark. "But you've caused me enough grief that I think I might enjoy some sport. The idiots down there have no clue what's going on, so we have a little bit of time to spare. I'll give you one free shot. Hit me anywhere you like. If I go down, I'll admit defeat."

Leopold knew it was a genuine offer. Stark really didn't think he could possibly lose. The consultant considered his opponent, tall and thickly built, and knew that his fists would be almost useless. He would need a better plan. The colonel holstered his weapon and beckoned him forward.

Leopold charged at Stark, trying to gain enough momentum in his body to lend extra weight to his attack. He clenched his right fist and threw it with as much force as he could manage at his opponent's exposed throat. Leopold felt Stark choke as the blow landed and watched him stumble backward, gagging for air. The consultant attacked again, making the most of the advantage he had just won, and aimed a kick at the colonel's groin, with the hope of putting him down. Before he could connect, his opponent lashed out with the back of his right hand and hit him across the face with enough force to knock him off course. Leopold stumbled and fell into a tree, hitting his head and falling to his knees. He looked up at Stark, who was laughing.

The camouflaged giant walked casually over and drew the handgun from his belt. He pulled the consultant to his feet with one hand and brought the butt of the gun across his skull with the other. Leopold felt like he'd been hit with a sledgehammer. Stark lashed out twice more, and the gun came away dripping with blood. Leopold felt hot liquid dripping down the side of his face and felt dizzy. His legs gave out underneath him, but his opponent's impossibly strong grip kept him held up. He knew it wouldn't be long now. There was only one more move to try.

He reached into his jacket pocket, fumbling awkwardly and trying to buy some time. Stark drew closer, his hot breath pounding against Leopold's face, not noticing what the consultant was doing with his hands. He was staring directly into Leopold's eyes. The huge assassin pushed his quarry up against the trunk of the tree and pulled out a large, curved knife from a sheath he had strapped to his shin, concealed underneath his clothes. From the many zip pockets Leopold could see, Stark could have any kind of arsenal hidden on his person. He held the knife to Leopold's left eye, bringing the tip of the blade close enough so that the consultant saw double. Stark sneered.

"If only we had a little more time on our hands, I'd like to have some more fun with you."

He edged the knife closer. It was touching the eyeball now. Leopold could feel the steel scratching against his cornea and tried not to flinch.

"Unfortunately," Stark continued, "I really do have to be on my way soon."

"I have a question for you," said Leopold, trying not to move.

His opponent paused, contemplating a response. Eventually, he relaxed the hand holding the knife and smiled. "I don't suppose it will make any difference now. Be quick."

"How did you manage it?" said Leopold, taking the opportunity to take a deep breath. "All the planning. All the political connections you would have needed. The money. How did you pull it off?"

Stark relaxed his grip a little further and pulled back the knife. Then he threw back his enormous shoulders and laughed.

"You honestly think I'm the biggest problem this country has to worry about? I'm just the tip of the iceberg."

"So it was someone else pulling the strings the whole time?" said Leopold.

"Just be thankful you'll never have the chance to find out."

"Give me a name," said the consultant, looking straight into Stark's eyes.

"Why? It won't matter. Nothing will save you now."

"I just want to die knowing who beat me."

Stark paused for a moment. "I don't suppose it'll make any difference," he said, bringing the knife up to Leopold's throat. "And it's always good to know when you are bested."

"Tell me."

The soldier leant forward and whispered a name into Leopold's ear. When he had finished, he drew away and tightened his grip.

"Now. How do you want to die?" asked Stark, holding up the steel blade. "Knife or bullet?"

"Bullet. Through the heart."

"Very well. At least you'll die with some honor."

Stark threw the consultant to the ground at his feet and kicked him in the ribs, rolling him a few feet back toward the clearing.

"Now, stand up," said the assassin, grinning as he pulled out his handgun.

Leopold complied, concealing his cell phone in the palm of his hand as he did so.

"Any last words?"

"Just one," said Leopold. "Duck."

Stark looked confused. Leopold dropped to the floor and hit the send button on his cell phone. The soldier's eyes widened in panic as he realized what had happened, frantically patting down the zip pockets that lined the front of his fatigues.

"What have you –" Stark began, but he never got to finish.

The two micro-explosives that Leopold had planted on Stark when he had been forced up against the tree received the signal from his cell phone and detonated. The consultant felt hot air blow against his face and he screwed up his eyes as the blast hit him, shielding himself with his hands and dropping to the ground as the shockwave hit. His ears rang from the noise, a wet thunderclap that was much louder than he had expected.

He looked up. Stark was still standing, a frozen look of surprise on his face. The colonel glanced down at his chest. Most of it was missing, exposing raw, dripping flesh and charred bone. Leopold could see where the man's rib cage and lungs had once been. He could make out the lower intestines, which had been ripped apart and were leaking a thick, yellow liquid.

Stark opened his mouth in a futile attempt to breathe before his eyes rolled back into his head and he crumpled to his knees, where he stayed for a few seconds until his dead muscles relaxed and he fell onto his front. His leg twitched and he lay still.

Cold air hit Leopold's lungs as he finally took a breath. His ribs flared in pain and he felt his head throb from where Stark had hit him. But he was alive. The ringing in his ears began to subside, and he could make out the sound of footsteps approaching through the woodland. Lots of footsteps.

He felt his vision began to darken and he knew he would pass out any second. His eyelids flickered. He could make out flashes of movement and noise and what he thought sounded like people talking. All of a sudden he was on his feet, hoisted up by an unknown force. Then the pain hit him again and his eyes snapped open, the world shifted into focus and his brain figured out what was going on.

"Leopold, can you hear me?" Jerome shouted into his ear.

The consultant grunted and looked around him. Six police officers and three Secret Service agents stood nearby, guns drawn, checking for danger. One of the police officers checked Stark's pulse, a futile exercise considering that most of the pulmonary system was missing, but protocol nonetheless. Another officer checked the colonel's body for any hidden weapons. The three Secret Service agents looked at Leopold with curiosity and holstered their firearms.

"What you two did was pretty stupid," said one of the agents. "But I've got to give you credit for getting the job done."

Leopold stared at the agent. Now was the time for damage control. The Secret Service would brief the FBI, who would quickly put up a cover story in case any of the details went public. Leopold doubted he would come off well in the report.

"Area secure," one of the police officers shouted.

The agent nodded and ordered one of the others to call in the medical and forensic teams. Then all three agents stalked off in the direction of the funeral procession. Jerome wrapped Leopold's arm around his shoulder and began walking after them. The police officers busied themselves with cordoning off the scene.

"What happened?" asked Jerome.

"After the Secret Service took you out, I went to find Stark. I wanted to trail him. Unfortunately, he saw me coming."

"How did you manage to cause so much damage?"

"I was able to plant the remaining explosives on him while he was preoccupied. Then I just had to hope I'd get the opportunity to get far enough back to detonate them."

"Risky move."

Leopold nodded and felt the bodyguard pick up the slack as more of the strength in his legs left him.

"Mary called," said Jerome. "She's on her way in one of the ambulances. I texted her to say you were okay once I eventually found my cell. Had to pry it out of Christina's hands."

"There was one other thing," said the consultant, weakly.

"What's that?"

Leopold told him what Stark had said during their encounter.

"Someone else was calling the shots?" said the bodyguard, once his employer had finished. "Did you get a name?"

"Yes. And it's not a name I ever thought I would hear again."

Leopold felt his legs buckle again. He managed to summon enough strength to keep from collapsing and told Jerome the name the colonel had whispered into his ear.

"That's impossible. He's lying. He must be."

"Why would he lie? He was just about to kill me."

"Maybe he just felt like messing with you one last time."

"No. I heard it in his voice. He was telling the truth."

Jerome didn't press the point any further, but Leopold could tell he was worried. A few minutes later they reached the funeral procession. The President had gone, rushed away by the Secret Service, and the rest of the mourners were now back on their feet, many of them wearing confused and worried expressions. They eventually found Christina, who had claimed a seat near her father's casket. She looked up as they approached.

"My father always told me that the legacy a person leaves is the only inheritance that matters," said Christina, tears welling in her eyes. "But he's left me nothing but pain and humiliation. How can I ever forgive him?"

"Maybe you don't need to," said Leopold, sitting down next to Christina. "Your father's legacy will hang over your head for the rest of your life. It will shape you and your family forever. And, more importantly, your father's legacy will make you work harder than ever to prove to the world that you are not like him. You can achieve amazing things with the right motivation, Christina. I have a feeling we can expect great things from you."

She smiled weakly and began to sob. He put his arm around her, and the three of them sat in silence. After a few minutes, Leopold heard ambulance sirens approaching from a distance and got to his feet.

"Let's get out of here," said Leopold. "I don't have the energy to answer questions. We've got enough medical supplies at home to fix me up."

"What about Mary?" said Jerome.

"I'll call her later. I've got work to do."

The consultant stood and began to walk shakily away, in the opposite direction to the sound of the sirens. Jerome said goodbye to Christina and followed close behind. He called for a car to pick them up from the west entrance.

"What if Stark was just messing with you?" said the bodyguard, catching up.

"What if he wasn't? Only a handful of people on the planet know that name and what it means. And if it *is* true, we've got a lot more trouble coming our way. This won't be the last of it."

The bodyguard put his heavy hand on Leopold's shoulder and turned him around. "Don't let this get to you. Whatever happens, we'll be ready."

Leopold nodded. He knew his old friend was right. There was very little he could do for the moment. He could make out the cemetery gates now; just a few more minutes of excruciating pain and he wouldn't have to walk anywhere again for a while. When he was feeling up to it, he might even give Mary a call and see if she wanted to have dinner, assuming she forgave him for ditching her. He gave himself even odds.

In the meantime, there was a soft bed and hard liquor waiting for him at home, a tried and tested cure for broken bones and head trauma. The thought of spending some time off the grid brought a smile to Leopold's face, despite the pain in his ribs and the throbbing in his head. He was looking forward to a well-earned rest; but in the back of his mind he knew it wouldn't last long.

Epilogue

His real name was a secret that many had died to protect. And he was furious. It wasn't supposed to happen like this; there was no room for failure. He could feel the anger welling in his stomach, he could feel his jaw clench and his teeth grind as his fists shook with uncontrollable rage.

All the planning. All the money. Stealing state secrets and military prototypes was not an activity undertaken without serious commitment. All the time spent perfecting the plan for every contingency, and he had failed in one thing. He had underestimated the enemy. This was not a mistake that he would make again.

He drew a deep breath and let the anger leave his body. It wasn't a productive response right now. He remembered Sun Tzu and repeated the lesson over and over in his mind. *The supreme art of war is to subdue the enemy without fighting.*

He felt his pulse slow and his breathing return to normal. Now was not the time for anger. Now was the time to press his advantage. He went to his desk and sat down at the computer, finding the telephone number he needed in seconds. He dialed the number and the call went through. He heard someone answer on the third ring.

"Leopold Blake speaking," said the voice on the other end of the phone.

He paused before replying, letting the moment sink in. *Know thy self, know thy enemy. A thousand battles, a thousand victories.* He lifted the receiver closer to his lips and spoke, deep and clear.

"Hello, son."

THE END

SAMPLE

DEPARTED
A Leopold Blake Thriller

Chapter 1

A human body plummeting from a cruising altitude of thirty-five thousand feet takes three minutes to hit the ground. Low pressure and lack of oxygen cause loss of consciousness for most of the fall, until the last minute or so, where the average person will wake up just in time to see the ground hurtling toward them at over one hundred and twenty miles per hour. Not a pleasant way to die.

Leopold's mind swam with a variety of horrific scenarios as he squeezed his eyes shut even tighter and gripped the armrest of his seat. The flight had been largely uneventful, but the recent bout of rough turbulence over Newfoundland had shaken his nerves.

"Are you okay?" a soft, calm voice asked.

Leopold opened his eyes and glared at police sergeant Mary Jordan, one of the NYPD's finest, who hadn't stopped fussing over him since they sat down. He regretted not seating her in coach.

"I'll be fine," said Leopold harshly. "When you're as familiar with aerospace engineering as I am; it's impossible not to be concerned about the thousands of tiny things that could go wrong and drop us out of the sky."

"Fine, be like that," said Mary, turning back to her magazine. "But we've got another five hours before we land in London, and I'd rather not spend the entire flight with you in this mood."

The consultant grunted and gripped his armrest a little tighter. The first class cabin of the brand new Dreamliner 787 was state-of-the-art and spacious, but the tasteful luxury did nothing to calm Leopold's nerves. He waved to one of the flight attendants, who brought him another glass of Scotch. Downing the healthy measure, he felt the musky heat rise in the back of his throat. He exhaled slowly and sank into his chair.

This respite didn't last long.

"You must have some idea why we've been called out to Scotland Yard," said Mary, twisting to face Leopold over the partition that separated their seats. "The London Metropolitan Police have their pick of local forensic and criminology experts. Why bring in someone else from the US?"

The consultant sighed deeply. "Because I'm the best at what I do."

"And so modest," said Mary, her finely sculpted features settling into a smile. "But why bring me along?"

"My contract is with the FBI, and they're leaning on your boss for extra resources. Apparently they can't spare anyone at the moment, which is where the NYPD comes in."

The police sergeant rolled her eyes. "So I'm just the babysitter?"

"That all depends on what we find when we get there. Scotland Yard refused to give me any details on the case. We're going in blind."

"Let's make sure we play this one by the book," said Mary, sitting back in her chair. "We don't want to make the FBI look bad, now, do we?"

Leopold was sure he detected a note of sarcasm, but chose not to press the matter.

"You must be expecting trouble if you've brought him," said Mary, pointing to Jerome, who was watching their conversation from the back of the first class section.

"Wherever I go, Jerome goes," said Leopold. "In my line of work, it pays to have personal protection at all times. Plus, he's been with me for more than twenty years, so I don't think he's about to quit now."

"Does he ever sleep?" asked Mary.

"I think so. But I've never seen it myself."

Leopold grinned and turned to look at Jerome, who sat serenely in his chair, itself barely large enough to contain his muscular frame. The giant bodyguard was dressed in his usual elegant Armani suit, blended almost perfectly to match his coal-black skin, and was wearing a set of Sennheiser headphones that Leopold suspected weren't connected to anything.

"Just make sure your head is in the game," said Mary, concern registering in her voice as Leopold turned back to face the front. "After what happened, I can understand if you're not one hundred percent."

"Drop it, Mary," said Leopold, closing his eyes and leaning back in his chair. "It's late and I need to be at my best when we arrive in London."

He heard Mary sit back in her own chair again with a resigned sigh. Keeping his eyes closed, he let the gentle thrum of the aircraft's engines take over, the sound lulling him to sleep within a few minutes. As the aircraft cruised across the Atlantic, Leopold shuffled uncomfortably in his seat, his dreams flitting in and out, amid flashes of broken memories from a childhood he couldn't quite remember.

CHAPTER 2

The early morning was colder and wetter than usual, and the moon provided only limited illumination as the hunter stalked the cobblestone paths that wound through the ancient city. London was a maze of densely packed alleyways and side streets, especially in the east of the city where he had chosen to spend his nights, and there were plenty of shadows and sheltered recesses that could be used to his advantage. It was still several hours until dawn, but only a few minutes until last call at the several dozen pubs and bars that lined the more well-lit areas, meaning his prey would venture outside soon.

The case he carried had room for sixteen knives, and it was full. He had lovingly sharpened each blade by hand earlier in the evening, placing them in the case in order of size – ranging from the tiny paring knife all the way to the butcher's cleaver. They were all strapped in tight and rolled up, making it easy and discreet to carry them around in public. Thanks to the predictable English weather, he didn't look out of place wearing the transparent raincoat, which meant there would be no need to burn his clothes afterwards. The surgical gloves would stay in his pocket for the time being.

Crossing to the end of the street, he stood in one of the pools of shadow that had formed just out of reach of the streetlights, keeping his eyes locked on the pub on the opposite side of the road. The King's Head looked dreary from the outside, but there was a considerable crowd within, all laughing and drinking away their lives, sheltered from the miserable weather outside. Within seconds, he caught sight of his prey as she passed by the window and allowed himself a smile. Soon, her suffering would be over.

Several minutes passed and the pub's lights dimmed, signaling closing time. The front doors opened and the merrymakers began to pour out into the soggy streets, fumbling for their umbrellas and hoods as the fat rain caught them by surprise. His target followed at the rear, trying to catch the attention of the young men who had dawdled. She looked a little off her game tonight.

After a few minutes she gave up, slurring something inaudible at the last youth as he backed away and walked off with his hands stuffed into his pockets. Wavering slightly on the spot, the young woman leaned up against the pub's dingy walls for support. Eventually regaining her balance, she slung her tiny handbag over a bare shoulder and hugged herself against the cold.

The hunter caught her eye as she crossed the street, and she smiled at him. Stepping out into the light, he took her by the hand. She didn't flinch. After a few minutes they reached a more secluded part of the neighborhood, and he chose a sheltered spot where nobody would be able to see. She mentioned something about payment, and then began to put her hands on him. He resisted the urge to vomit in her face as the whore's skin touched his own, instead pretending to reach for his wallet. The bitch's breath stank of alcohol.

Pulling the surgical gloves out of his pocket and slipping them on his hands, the whore said it would be extra for the kinky stuff. He wanted to wrap his hands around her throat and squeeze until the larynx popped, but he knew he had to be patient. Methodical. There was an art to this that had to be respected. Inhaling deeply, he pushed the thought to the back of his mind. The bitch asked about payment again.

His hand moved too quickly for her to register what happened next. The polished blade the killer carried in his pocket was light and strong, and he whipped the razor-sharp edge across the young woman's throat in one smooth motion, then again in the opposite direction. Nothing happened for a second or two, and then the blood came. First in slow drips and then faster, the arterial pressure forcing the two wounds to open wider, spraying his waterproof coat with hot, red liquid.

The hunter licked his lips slowly, tasting the familiar copper flavor as some of the blood coated his face. The whore's eyes were wide with shock, but there was no chance of her screaming as she crumpled slowly to the floor. The bitch even tried to grab at his raincoat for support, but it was slick with blood and no use to her. Within a few seconds she lost consciousness and lay still, her breathing shallow and weak.

Time to go to work, the killer's mind buzzed as his excitement reached fever pitch.

He knelt and unrolled the case, selecting his favorite blade: a sturdy, six-inch knife with a carbon-fiber edge and excellent balance, and cut open her dress at the hem to reveal her naked body. Ignoring the fact she wasn't wearing underwear, he focused his attention on the exposed stomach area, using his fingers to detect where the first cut should be made. Satisfied, he slipped the knife's tip into her skin, peeling it apart with ease and opening a tear in her soft, white abdomen. There was very little blood left.

His heart pounded with excitement as her last breath drifted slowly into the night.

Now for the fun part.

Chapter 3

Leopold snapped awake as the Dreamliner hit the runway and the jet engines threw themselves into reverse. He grabbed his armrest with renewed vigor as the forces acting on the aircraft caused the cabin to tilt and sway as they slowed. Within a few seconds the plane had settled into a gentle taxi, and he allowed himself to relax a little.

"Interesting dreams?" asked Mary, unbuckling her seatbelt and stretching out. "You were muttering something in your sleep for most of the flight. Couldn't make out a word."

"Don't remember," lied the consultant, yawning. "Probably nothing exciting."

The arrivals process at Heathrow proved surprisingly painless, and Leopold, Mary, and Jerome collected their luggage without issue and made their way though to the arrivals lounge. The consultant spotted the young driver from Scotland Yard, who was dressed in civilian clothes and holding a placard.

"No black cab?" said Mary, as they approached their contact and shook hands.

"No, ma'am," said their contact, smiling. "That's just the cabbies. Sergeant Cooper, at your service."

"Pleasure," said Mary, looking the sergeant up and down.

"No uniform, Sergeant?" said Leopold, as Cooper started to lead them in the direction of the parking lot.

"No, sir. I'm part of the – um," – he stuttered slightly – "case you're here to help with. The superintendent will fill you in when we get back to the Yard."

"Your accent, Cooper," said Leopold. "Not from around here, are you?"

"No, sir. Transfer from South Yorkshire police. Came down two weeks ago specifically to work on – well, you'll find out soon. Here we are."

The sergeant opened the rear passenger door of the black Audi A4 sedan and gestured for Leopold and Jerome to climb in. He held the front door open for Mary before packing the luggage into the trunk and settling himself into the driver's seat. Leopold winced slightly as he nestled into the chilly leather and hoped the car would warm up quickly.

"It's gone lunch time, have you eaten?" asked Cooper, turning his head toward Leopold.

"Not in a while. I'd prefer to wait until we've been briefed before thinking about a meal, if you wouldn't mind."

"Speak for yourself," muttered Mary.

"No problem, sir," said Cooper. "We should be there in forty minutes or so, traffic allowing. If you have any questions, I'll do my best to answer them on the way."

Jerome sat forward. "Who knows we're here?"

"Not too many people," said Cooper, easing the car out of the line of slow traffic and into the bus lane. "The superintendent, the commissioner, and some of the top brass from the FBI are all aware of your flight plan. Other than that, I don't have the clearance, so I couldn't tell you."

"You'll draw too much attention using this lane during busy traffic," said Jerome. "What if we're stopped?"

"The number plate, sorry – license plate, is linked to the Met police database. Any problems and my clearance flashes up. Don't worry, I've been trained to keep you safe."

"Where do you keep your firearm?" said Jerome, ignoring Cooper's last comment.

"Not licensed to carry, I'm afraid," said the sergeant. "Which reminds me, while you're on British soil you'll have to remain unarmed. I hope that won't be a problem."

Leopold felt Jerome tense slightly and could have sworn the temperature in the car fell by a few degrees.

"I keep a Taser with me at all times," continued the Yorkshireman. "If we run into any trouble, there's enough power in one of those to put down a baby elephant."

"Fine," said Jerome, his voice flat. "I'll need to conduct a full security assessment before we go out in the field, if you could arrange that for us upon arrival."

"No problem," said Cooper, easing the car forward a little faster. "Won't be long now."

The rest of the journey passed in silence, other than the occasional question from Mary regarding the scenery as they cruised through the suburbs and into the heart of the city. Leopold noticed most of the famous landmarks as they reached the Thames river, and Cooper filled in the gaps when Mary pointed out buildings she didn't recognize.

They eventually reached Westminster, where they left the highway and joined the line of traffic that snaked through the upmarket streets, lined on either side with glass-fronted office buildings, Georgian apartment blocks, and gleaming department stores flying the Union Jack at full mast. The black Audi sailed past most of the stationary vehicles, slowing only as they were joined by the epitomic red double-decker buses that shared the empty lanes. Cooper pulled away from the main road as one of the bus drivers blasted his horn in irritation, steering the car down one of the side roads that led up to the headquarters of the Metropolitan Police.

Leopold spotted the iconic New Scotland Yard wedge-shaped sign, familiar from countless news reports and detective shows, spinning slowly on its axis as the sergeant pulled the Audi around to the secured parking lot. An officer wearing a high-visibility jacket checked Cooper's identification and waved them through the security checkpoint, down into the basement structure.

"Might not be here much longer," said the Yorkshireman, peering through the gloom for a parking space. "The Met is considering selling the place next year and moving us to Whitechapel. Probably quite fitting, given the current situation."

The consultant nodded absentmindedly and pointed out a free space near the elevators. "Will Superintendent Swanson be seeing us soon? It's been a long trip."

"Oh yes, he knows you're here," said Cooper, lining up the car and reversing into the space. "I'll take you up to his office straight away."

Leopold stepped out into the parking lot and followed Cooper to the elevators, where the four of them rode up to the sixth story offices. The sergeant led them through the stuffy corridors until they reached Swanson's office, where he knocked and opened the door.

Superintendent Swanson sat behind a large, wooden desk, and was scribbling something on a piece of notepaper as Leopold stepped through into the office. Swanson was middle-aged, perhaps forty-five, and almost completely gray-haired, including his substantial moustache. He wore a stylish but conservative suit and stood up as the sergeant closed the door behind him.

"Ah, Mr Blake and companions," said the superintendent, his thick voice booming across the room. "So glad to finally meet you."

Leopold shook Swanson's hand, who gripped a little harder than the consultant had expected, before taking a seat across the desk. Cooper offered Jerome and Mary a seat on the small sofa at the back of the office, where they would still be able to join in the conversation.

"Thank you, Cooper," said Swanson, taking his seat. "I'll update you later."

Leopold saw the sergeant nod politely and leave the room. The superintendent's office was large enough to seat a half-dozen people, and had a generous view of the quiet streets below. The thick, reflective windows filtered the light somewhat, giving the outside world an odd hue that somehow made the interior of the building feel as overcast as the city itself.

"I understand you haven't yet been briefed," said Swanson, interlocking his fingers.

"Not yet," said Leopold. "But I have a few theories as to why we're here."

"Really?" said Swanson, leaning forward. "I was told about your particular talents. I'd be interested to hear what you've managed to figure out already."

The consultant heard Mary shift her weight on the sofa behind him, and knew without looking that she was probably rolling her eyes.

"With pleasure," said Leopold. "The Metropolitan Police are among the finest in the world, with access to almost unlimited resources. However, like many organizations, they will gladly outsource where they feel it is required. In this case you've called in the FBI, which suggests you suspect a foreign involvement."

"Good, good," said Swanson, his eyes twinkling. "Go on."

"Naturally, the FBI are woefully under-resourced and decided to use one of their consultants instead of sending out a team. That's where I come in."

"Very astute," said the superintendent. "Anything else?"

"It's unlikely the FBI would get involved for anything less than a homicide case," said Leopold. "So I had assumed we would be assisting with a murder enquiry. Once Ms. Jordan got involved, my suspicions were confirmed. The NYPD doesn't send out one of its top homicide detectives without reason, even if they do want to keep an eye on me."

Leopold turned to look at Mary, who was shifting uncomfortably on the sofa next to Jerome, whose large frame took up most of the space.

"Very good, Mr Blake," said Swanson, beaming.

"I'm not done yet," said the consultant, raising a finger. "Your man Cooper isn't what he seems."

"What do you mean?" asked the superintendent, his smile fading.

"A transfer from another police force to assist with a particular case is unusual, especially for someone with a mere sergeant's rank. His car was brand new, a luxury model, which someone on his salary would be unlikely to afford. It's not a rental, either. His accent was a little jumbled, suggesting someone who had lived away from home for several years, not a person who had just arrived in the last few weeks. All of which suggests to me that Cooper doesn't work in your department. What's his involvement with this case?"

Swanson sighed heavily. "Cooper doesn't work for me, at least not directly. I can't tell you more than that."

Leopold sat in silence for several seconds before replying. "I'm sorry, Superintendent. I can't assist if you won't be forthright with me." He stood and turned to leave.

"Mr. Blake, wait," said Swanson, getting to his feet. "Please, sit down." He gestured to the empty chair.

"Two weeks ago, the FBI informed us that one of their persons of interest had landed on British soil," said Swanson, settling back into his chair as

Leopold reluctantly sat down again. "He's wanted for questioning in connection with a spree of murders in his hometown of Portland, Oregon. No arrest warrant yet, which is why he managed to get on a plane, but we have a longstanding agreement with the US authorities to keep each other well informed. An agreement like that, between two foreign nations, does not go unchecked."

"Understood," said Leopold. "Which means that if Cooper doesn't work here, and this is a case of national security, I assume he's MI5?"

"Of course, I can't confirm that," said Swanson, avoiding eye contact. "But I can assure you that he's been thoroughly vetted and will provide invaluable support during this investigation. He also has contacts within Whitehall that could prove useful."

"Fine," said Leopold. "Has this person of interest been detained?"

"No. Cooper can't approach him in case his cover is blown, and we need to keep him incognito, you understand. We actually have no legal grounds to keep the man locked up without solid evidence, which is why we need some help. Off the books, you understand."

"Naturally," said Leopold, leaning back in his chair. "What's the man's name?"

"Kandinski. George Kandinski."

"And I assume you are under the impression he is responsible for a homicide on British soil?"

"Precisely, old boy. We got the red flag that he had touched down just a few days before we find a body with injuries closely matching the MO of the Portland killer. A week later we find another one, and a body was found early this morning that we think is linked also.

That's three murders already – that we know about, anyway. There may be more. If Kandinski's the one responsible, we need to bring him in before he does any more damage."

"Do you have anything tying him to the crimes?" said the consultant, fixing his eyes on the superintendent.

"Well, that's the problem," said Swanson. "There isn't anything linking him to any crime within British borders, nor any international warrant for his arrest. We can bring him in for questioning, but he'll have to be released after twenty-four hours if we can't convince the Crown Prosecution Service to bring charges. Even sooner if he gets hold of a good solicitor. We need some solid evidence linking him to the killings."

"And you want me to find it?"

"Exactly."

"I'll need to know more about the case," said Leopold. "Assuming the three deaths were homicide, I'll need to examine the bodies."

"They are most definitely homicides," said Swanson. "You can take a look at the bodies. I'll take you down to the morgue right now, it's not far."

"Excellent. Lead the way."

Swanson stood up and made for the door before pausing. "Have you had lunch yet?"

"No. That's the second time I've been asked that question," said Leopold. "If you insist, we can grab a bite to eat on the way."

"No, it's not that," said the superintendent, opening the door. "Its just that I would strongly recommend having an empty stomach for this one."

END OF SAMPLE

For details of where to buy the full book, as well as updates, news, and promotions, simply visit the author's website at www.nickstephensonbooks.com